SWEET TEA

By

Wendy Lynn Decker

Serenity Books
http://www.wendylynndeckerauthor.com
Email: serenitybookpublishing@aol.com

ISBN 978-1499180152

Book front and back cover concept and design by, Larissa Spathis and Calogero Panzardi.

Also by Wendy Lynn Decker, THE BEDAZZLING BOWL

Dedication: To my mother.

The cardinal is a sign of hope from a loved one who has passed. When you see one, it means they are visiting you. The cardinal usually shows up when you miss your loved one that has passed or during times of celebration as well as despair to let you know they will always be with you.

CHAPTER 1

Mama was different from other mothers, only I didn't realize *how* different, until the day she buried our Thanksgiving turkey in the front yard. At the time, Mama believed the sacrificial act would save our sinful souls. In actuality, it challenged me to sacrifice my own.

I'd been waiting around the house all day for the big feast. Mama had put the turkey in the oven early that morning, and it was near sundown. The smell of sausage balls and sweet potato pie lingered in the air making my mouth water and stomach growl. Luke, my twelve-year-old brother wore a face that told me if he didn't get fed soon, he might go hunting in the backwoods. But, he didn't say anything, which was very unlike him. My older sister, CeCe, didn't seem to care one way or the other. Like always, I nominated myself to find out what was going on. Like always, I discovered more than I bargained for.

"Mama, where's the turkey?" I said. "It's been in the oven all darn day. I'm starving."

She sprung up from the couch nearly knocking me off my feet. I jumped back.

"You wanna know where the turkey is, Olivia? I'll show you where the turkey is." She stormed out the front door and down the aluminum staircase, and stepped over the short picket fence into the tiny garden in front of our trailer home. She fell to her knees and ripped through the dirt and rose bushes with her bare hands. Strands of dark hair clung to her pale face. I watched in confused horror, shivering in the fear of not knowing what she was about to do.

She stood up, holding something in her arms. Grass and mud covered her clothes, smeared mascara darkened her high cheekbones, and the eyes of a stranger glared at me; a stranger I had met before. With outstretched arms, she stepped forward and shoved a fifteen-pound cooked turkey at me.

I backed away from the defiled bird. "It's okay, Mama, we don't need to eat turkey. . . . Heck, I don't even like turkey! CeCe, c'mere," I shouted.

My sixteen-year-old mind was used to what we called "Mama's quirks," but this was the worst yet.

I stood motionless. CeCe rushed to my side. Wide-eyed, she stared at Mama for a second and then spoke to her in a calm voice. "What's going on here, Mama? What are you doing with the turkey?"

"Tell her, Olivia, tell her!" Mama hollered as she dangled the bird by one hind leg at her side.

I couldn't tell CeCe if I wanted to because I hadn't a clue why Mama would bury our Thanksgiving turkey in the first place.

"I did it for us." She dropped the turkey onto the ground and started to cry. "We haven't been livin' right for the Lord, but now He will not forsake us."

She began a babbling chant. "*Jai . . . Guru . . . Deva . . . Om. Jai . . . Guru . . . Deva . . . Om.* Hold my hand, Olivia, say it with me . . . *Jai Guru Deva . . .*"

Leaving the turkey where she'd dropped it, CeCe took Mama's scratched and dirty hand and led her to the front door. Mama reached for mine with her other hand. I grabbed it and trailed behind.

"What's she saying?" I whispered.

"She's singing that John Lennon song Daddy used to play for her on guitar." CeCe gazed toward the sky and we chanted along with Mama as we led her into the house. "*Nothing's gonna change my world . . ."*

CeCe pressed on Mama's shoulders so she'd sit down, and I lifted a pillow from the couch and placed it behind her head.

My brother Luke peered at Mama with a narrow stare. "Where's the turkey, and when are we eatin'?"

"Just forget about the turkey," I hissed.

"I'm hungry." Luke yanked the refrigerator door open. He stared for a minute, and then slammed it shut. "Ain't never nothing in this house to eat."

Luke flew off into his bedroom, probably to dismantle his TV for the hundredth time. Daddy used to say Luke leaped out of Mama's womb and right into his toolbox. Daddy died in a car crash on December 8th. The same date Mama's beloved John Lennon was shot and killed. Daddy was the only man Mama loved more than John. It devastated her; it devastated all of us.

In a few weeks it would be the fourth anniversary of Daddy's death. The bizarre connection to John Lennon continued to twist Mama's mind and hinder our healing. It also sabotaged our holiday season.

Although we all suffered the loss of Daddy, I felt as if CeCe and Luke suffered the most. I was like the extra child on a wooden seesaw shifting from side-to-side; sometimes by Luke, other times by Mama. Splinters pricked me, wore me out,

4

tempted me to hop off. I learned to pluck them with tweezers from God's first-aid kit.

"Don't worry, Luke, we'll eat turkey, just not right now," CeCe said, and pulled a glass from the cupboard. "I'll pour you some sweet tea, Mama. Tea always makes you feel good."

Mama sat quietly staring into space. Out of the corner of my eye, I saw CeCe grab a bottle of pills from the cupboard. She poured the tea into the glass and opened two capsules and slipped the contents into the glass and stirred.

"Here Mama, drink your tea." She held the glass to Mama's lips. She took a sip. After about four more sips, Mama placed the glass on the end table.

Not long after, she fell asleep.

"What did you do?" I whispered.

"I bought sleeping pills from the pharmacy. It won't hurt her. It'll just make her sleep for a while. She hasn't slept in days. Haven't you noticed?"

"I noticed," I said. "You think I don't hear her clanking dishes at the kitchen sink in the middle of the night, or blasting the TV while she watches those weirdo shows?"

Mama battled with sleep all the time. She slept either too much or too little. There was never an in-between with Mama in anything she did. Even when it came to God. Mama loved Him with all her heart or she wanted nothing to do with Him. We all followed suit with her decision to forget Him after Daddy died. However, lately, I found myself praying again. Mostly for Mama, that she would meet a nice man who'd take care of her. Then I wouldn't have to worry if CeCe left. The closer she came to graduating Landon Community College, the more frequent my prayers became.

CeCe grabbed her purse and sprinted for the front door.

"Where ya goin'?" I said. My heart quickened. I didn't want her to leave. What if Mama woke up and did something worse? She'd done many unusual things over the past few years, but this incident brought Mama's quirks to a new level of peculiarity. I followed CeCe outside to her car.

"Go back inside," she said. "I'm just going to the store for some food."

She turned to get into the car, and I noticed a streak of dirt above her upper lip. I laughed. Sometimes I had to laugh after things settled down with Mama. Perhaps it was a nervous laugh, but it beat crying, and I had done enough of that after Daddy died.

"What in the world are you laughing at?" CeCe asked, annoyed.

"Hold still." I stretched the sleeve of my sweatshirt over

my thumb and wiped away her dirt mustache. "You can't go anywhere like that."

She bent down and checked her face in the car's side mirror then pointed toward the garden. "Throw that turkey in the trash, will ya?" She took off.

Back inside, Luke stared at the TV.

"Where'd she go?" he whispered.

I reached inside my pocket and pulled out a piece of bubblegum. "Here," I tossed it to him. "She went to get some food, it's gonna be all right," I told him, although I had no idea if it would be.

Mama still lay asleep on the couch. Her deep breaths turned into heavy snores. She looked helpless. Not like a mother. Like someone who needed a mother, and seeing her that way filled my loneliness with more invisible pain.

After Daddy's death, CeCe and I accepted Mama's depression as natural. But weeks turned into months, and months into years, and it seemed as if Mama's grief transformed itself into another being who took up residence inside of her head. I never knew which one I'd be seeing from day-to-day.

Fifteen minutes later, CeCe returned. The three of us ate a Thanksgiving dinner of turkey pot pies, macaroni and cheese, and chocolate pudding for dessert. After we finished, we sat at the table and stared at one another. I spoke up first. "Shouldn't we call Grandma and Grandpa?"

CeCe shrugged. "No sense in calling them. It's not like it'll make a difference."

Mama's parents, Lily May and Charles Cleveland lived in a retirement village in Texas. They only came to visit when the spirit moved them, and it hadn't since Daddy's funeral. Daddy would have been surprised to see Grandma and Grandpa. We hardly saw them when they lived in Georgia, and I don't remember him being very fond of them.

"What about Aunt Nadine?" I suggested.

CeCe raised her right eyebrow. "Whatever for? She'll never leave her fancy apartment in New York City to come down here and help her *quirky sister Cassandra.*"

I often dreamed I could move in with Aunt Nadine and wear designer clothes and expensive perfume. I'd stroll down the streets of New York City and people would stare at me because they wanted to be me, not because they wanted me to go away. Even though I was born there, I had only seen New York City on TV and in movies.

But CeCe was right. The only time we heard from Aunt Nadine was when we received the generous check inside the self-portrait Christmas card she sent us each year or on some rare occasion.

"How about What's His Name?" I asked.

CeCe raised both eyebrows at the mention of Mama's brother. "You can't even remember his name, why would we call him?"

The truth was, no one had been there for us after Daddy died. It had always been CeCe, and she'd been preparing me for the fact that she'd be leaving soon. "I'm not staying in Landon, Georgia all my life," she often told me. "Soon as I save enough money and finish school, I'm boarding a plane for Hollywood."

Back in high school, CeCe held the lead in all the school plays. Mama swore she would be famous one day. Mama would raise her chin, pull her shoulders back and strut around town, bragging about CeCe to anyone who'd listen. It made me crazy jealous.

I wasn't sure what I wanted for my future. It was difficult to focus on one that included juggling life with Mama. Heck, it was hard enough to live my life the way most sixteen year olds did, or for that matter, take charge when CeCe was worn out and Mama was incapable of just being her own self. But I knew for sure I didn't want to stay in Landon any more than CeCe did. I wanted a career—something I could be proud of—something where people would be proud of me. Although Mama talked of

CeCe becoming an actress, I knew she would die if CeCe left, and *I* would never have a chance to live. I needed to find a way to make her stay.

CHAPTER 2

"Did you kill her?" I nervously picked a clump of mascara from my eyelashes and wiped it on my black jeans. Then I flipped the snap at the waistband open to keep my pants from digging into my waist so I could breathe a little easier. My heart, a firecracker about to blow. I didn't want her to be dead, but I didn't want her to be alive in the same state of mind she'd been, and I felt insurmountable guilt about those feelings.

Cece placed her finger above Mama's upper lip. "She's alive."

The firecracker sizzled out. My breath a steady pace. I followed Cece into the kitchen. Dressed in sweat pants and an NYU t-shirt, no make-up and her dark hair tied back with a rubber band, she still looked better than I did at my very best.

The toaster handle popped up and she pulled out two pieces

of bread. "Want some?"

I shook my head, no. "Don't you worry about anything?"

CeCe seemed so steady. Too steady. "I think you'd make a better surgeon than an actress," I said. "You could probably perform open-heart surgery with a slice of cherry pie next to the operating table without so much as a wave of nausea."

Cece buttered her bread and spoke without meeting my eyes. "You've got to be just as disciplined to be an actress as you do a doctor. It's just different that's all."

Suddenly, Mama's voice trailed in. "*I'd* like some toast please."

Cece grinned. "Sure, Mama. Butter or jelly?"

Mama acted as if nothing had happened. Like she never sacrificed our Thanksgiving dinner to the worms and grubs in the front yard so the Lord would save our souls. Even if Mama was in her right mind, I believed the Lord had already forgiven me when I was ten and baptized behind the pulpit at Landon Baptist Church. Though I hadn't been there for some time, now I feared my relationship with God might be in jeopardy.

I hadn't been picking up around the house as much as I should have. My constant scheming about keeping CeCe from pursuing her dreams so I could find mine would not make God proud. I figured my thoughts about sex most definitely didn't sit right with God. Sometimes I wanted to shake Mama and say, "What kind of clock makes you tick?" It sure isn't a Rolex. Maybe a Timex—an old one. One that got splashed in the kitchen sink too many times.

Although CeCe took care of most things, she had no inclination of trying to find a way to fix Mama. As far as she was concerned, Mama was . . . as Mama is, and always would be. CeCe didn't want to upset Mama, and I didn't want to upset CeCe. Although she never said it, I believe she planned to let Mama's broken clock tick until its time would no longer be counted. And neither would my plans for a future.

Finding a way to leave home after high school without worrying about what would become of Mama consumed my thoughts. I was next in line to care for her, and though it was only fair to CeCe, I couldn't bare the thought of taking on that task. I suppose it seemed selfish, but it was more than that. Being a caretaker didn't come natural to me; it frightened the hell out of me.

When the Monday morning after Thanksgiving rolled around, I wondered if Mama had taken a bath yet? It wasn't like her to wallow in filth. She spent more time in the bath than a bar of soap, but I wasn't going to be the one to suggest she get in the tub. I needed to get myself ready for school. I had to look just right today.

"Have you heard Mama run the bath yet?" I asked CeCe.

"Nope." She answered, while scrubbing the kitchen table as if she hoped it would change colors. "She went to bed after me last night. Hopefully she took one after I fell asleep." She waved her hand in front of her nose. "By the way, what kind of shampoo are you putting in your hair? Last night I sneezed about ten times when you rolled onto my side of the bed."

"Jonzie gave it to me," I said.

CeCe looked at me funny. "You sure it's for humans? Knowing Jonzie, it might be some type of dog shampoo."

"No! Jonzie found a bunch of it in her basement. Her Daddy used to work for a big fragrance company. He has boxes and boxes of samples."

"Did you check the expiration date? I think it may have gone bad."

I shrugged. "Maybe we could save up for bunk-beds, then your nose won't be so close to my head."

CeCe kept scrubbing. "Don't worry, you'll have the bed to yourself soon enough."

Though I would have loved to have the bed to myself, I'd rather share it with CeCe for five more years than let her go away and leave me alone with Mama.

Just then, the bathroom door creaked open and Mama stepped out. I could see her clearly from the kitchen. There were no twists and turns in the trailer like there had been in our house. Just one straight hallway of metal covered in taupe-painted drywall, with a portrait of our family hanging crooked from a skinny nail halfway down.

Daddy would have been sad if he knew our portrait no longer sat on the fireplace mantle. He loved our house. He built it especially for our family. I remember him saying he made sure to build it big enough so we would never have to move. The only thing reminiscent of our old house now, was the flowerbed Mama made on the small plot of grass on the side of the trailer.

Dressed in her uniform, all fresh and clean, she said, "Good morning, girls."

Cece and I breathed identical sighs of relief. "Morning," we said.

Mama smoothed the sides of her hair while she sucked her lips inward, staring into the air as if it were a mirror. "What a beautiful fall day it is."

"Yes, Ma'am," CeCe said. "It sure is a beautiful day."

She grabbed a couple of chocolate chip cookies from the cookie jar and waved goodbye. "Don't forget to wake Luke up." She slipped out the front door like any other Monday. But I knew it wasn't any other Monday. It was one Monday closer to the anniversary of Daddy and John Lennon's death.

Each year when the anniversary drew near, John Lennon's face plastered every station on the television. I would often dive across the living room floor rushing to change the channel before Mama saw it. We all knew if Mama saw Lennon's fans clutching their candles while they sang *Give Peace a Chance* in Central Park, there would be no peace for us.

I feared that one day I would find Mama at the bus stop holding her own vigil right in front of the Woodlane Trailer Park sign. Candles surrounding her hollering, "Olivia come sit with me in honor of your daddy." I know Daddy loved John Lennon too, but I know he would not have approved of Mama taking it to this extent. But she didn't respond to any of our reasoning.

One year, she bought a bunch of Lennon's posters, rolled them up, stuck them into the ground and lit each one on fire. I nearly died when the neighbors called the police on her, who had become aware of Mama's quirks, and they didn't make a big issue of it. I wished God would take December 8th off the calendar like some hotels did with the thirteenth floor. That particular year topped them all.

* * *

After staying late at school to make up an algebra test, I

stepped off the bus at the entrance to the Woodlane Trailer Park. My boyfriend, Mattéo on my mind, I wasn't paying attention while I walked. Instead, I was imagining what it might be like to go all the way with Matt when I tripped on a crack in the middle of the road. My loose-leaf binder fell from my arms and tumbled to the ground. I bent to pick it up, and a blurred vision of what appeared to be Mama caught my eye. She strutted toward me like a model charging the runway.

"Olivia, darlin'," she yelled, waving her hand in the air. Wrapped in a stylish black fur coat that hung to her ankles, a red hat and shoes, she spun around as if photographers were snapping her picture.

I nearly swallowed my gum and then peered over my shoulder to make sure no one else saw her. It was one thing when the older neighbors witnessed her strange behavior. But I couldn't bear any remarks from the trailer-trouble on the bus.

"Well . . . what do you think?" she asked.

"Mama, where in the world did you get that coat?"

She pulled the collar to her neck and closed her eyes in ecstasy. "Don't ya love it?"

"Well, yeah, it's beautiful." I took my glove off and touched her sleeve.

She grinned and raised her penciled eyebrows. "It's a mink!

I got one for you, too." She held her hands in the air like the hostess of a game show. "Come on, I'll show ya."

I followed a few feet behind her and caught sight of Miss Ruth and Bubbles Clayton on their patio. The nosiest two ladies in the neighborhood. I heard them gossip about Mama many times. They said things like, "Cassandra Travis is as nutty as a pecan pie." Or "Cassandra Travis's mind is one quarter short of a dollar." I tried to think of Mama as an eccentric widow, or a woman who walked to the beat of her own drum. Comments like that made it harder.

A neck brace held Miss Ruth's head straight in the air, and she sat like a statue glued to her chair. It must have tortured her not to be able to turn her head to follow us.

"I think that woman's a Russian spy," Mama whispered in my ear.

"Good thing we're not Russian," I nervously joked.

Mama covered her mouth and giggled. "You're so funny, Olivia."

Seemed Miss Ruth was aching to catch a glimpse of one of our family members doing something unorthodox so she had something to gossip about. I heard her chair scrape across the concrete patio as she hobbled along to get a closer look.

Mama opened the front door and I stepped inside and

gasped. Five fur coats lay across our couch: a short white one with a zipper and hood, a mid-length silver, a full-length silver, a brown one, and a short black mink. All of them resembled those Aunt Nadine wore in some of the Christmas portraits she'd sent us.

Mama pointed to the mink. "Go ahead, try it on."

I pulled the coat off the sofa and caressed its silky fur against my cheek. I'd never touched a fur coat before. I inhaled the scent. It reeked of Channel No. 5. I was only familiar with the fragrance because Aunt Nadine sent a bottle of it to CeCe when she graduated high school; however, I knew she didn't have any left.

Mama stepped in front of me, took the coat from my hands and wrapped it around me while I slid my arms through the sleeves.

She giggled like a schoolgirl. "Look at you! That shiny, black mink brings out the golden highlights in your hair—and your eyes—they look like two lost pennies that have just been found. You look beautiful, Olivia." She pointed toward the hallway. "Go see yourself."

Excited, I rushed down the hallway to the bathroom, closed the door, and stared in the mirror. Turning from side to side, I admired my reflection. I grabbed a brush from the vanity and ran it through my hair. I felt glamorous, even a bit taller, and I looked smart. However, I reminded myself it was more important for me to sound smart.

After moving to Woodlane, I worked extra hard at that. My plan: to rid myself of all traces of my southern accent while establishing an *extensive vocabulary*. My guidance counselor said it would help my future. I agreed. Having been the best speller in my class since grade school gave me a head start. If only I knew where I was headed.

My moment in La-La Land ended when the front door slammed and CeCe screamed, "Oh my Lord! Where'd these coats come from?"

I rushed out from the bathroom, still dressed in the mink. CeCe's jaw dropped.

"That's right," Mama said, and tossed her dark waves over her right shoulder.

"What's right?" CeCe asked.

"Thank the Lord," Mama said.

"For the coats?"

"Of course. The Lord gave us these coats!" She held out the long silver one toward CeCe. "This is fox. Go ahead, try it on."

"I don't want to try it on." CeCe pushed the coat back at Mama. "It's barely cold out now and it only lasts for a month or so, anyway."

Mama dangled the coat at her hip. "I had a fur coat many years ago—when I lived in New York City—your great-grandma gave it to me." She shook her head. "Only, I have no idea what happened to it. I've wanted another one ever since."

Both CeCe and I gazed up at her, and at the same time said, "But Mama, you've got five!"

She ignored us. "Just put the coat on, CeCe."

I wondered why CeCe didn't want to try it on. Did she think she'd like it and have to give it back? Did she think Mama would want us to wear them out together and pretend we were sisters? She did enjoy pretending she was younger than her age and often put on our clothes and pranced around the house fishing for compliments. Aside from that, I wondered what great-grandma she was talking about.

She pushed the coat toward CeCe's arms. "Go ahead."

I caught a sparkle in CeCe's eyes. I could tell she was dying to try the coat on.

"Come on, now!" Mama coaxed. "Put it on."

CeCe put on the coat and stroked her left arm with the palm of her right hand, then straightened up and shoved her fists into the pockets. She wore that coat as if it were custom-made.

Mama jumped up and down. "You're gonna need a coat

like this when you become famous. All movie stars wear fur coats." She picked up the white jacket with the hood. "Try this one on, Livy. It's rabbit."

I wondered if Mama could ever picture me famous? I had no desire to become an actress like CeCe, but I didn't want to be known as the girl with middle-child syndrome either. After seeing myself in that coat I *could* envision being famous. For what? I still wasn't sure. Only I knew I'd better find out before CeCe left or it might be too late.

I slid the mink off and replaced it with the rabbit. Then CeCe tried on the mid-length silver one. The three of us exchanged coats, running back and forth to the bathroom mirror, giggling while Mama applauded.

"It's a Christmas present from God!" she said.

"How did God get these coats to you?" CeCe asked.

Mama shrugged. "They were lying on the ground and God's voice said, 'Merry Christmas!'"

CeCe stared at Mama, then at me. We knew those coats didn't come from God, but we didn't want to argue. We liked seeing Mama this happy. Even though I secretly feared she wandered into someone's house and stole them, CeCe and I wore the coats and fed Bubbles Clayton and Miss Ruth more delicious gossip.

A few months later, we found out Mama told one of the men from the nursing home where she worked that her car needed repair. He was always giving Mama money because he liked her, and said he had no family to give it to anyway. Only, when he gave her money to fix her car, her mind thought he said, *Buy some furs.* Even so, I figured she bought the coats used from an estate sale because they weren't new. But they sure were pretty.

Monica Bradshaw's jaw dropped like a fat squirrel from an oak tree the day I sauntered into homeroom wearing my new coat.

"Well look at you, Miss Trailer Queen, all wrapped up in a fur coat. Did your little brother catch it live and skin it for you too?" Luke had gone from a baseball-playing typical young boy to a back-woods hick since we'd moved to the trailer park, but insulting him like she did made my chest tight and face burn.

At first, I felt a spike of anger ready to thrust from my fist into Monica's button nose. Instead, I fluttered my lashes and held my head high. "No, Monica. Only your daddy would accomplish such a task by hand. I got this as a gift."

Monica's face reddened. I could almost see smoke whistling from her ears as her mind spun fast trying to outwit me. Regardless of her standing as Landon's golden girl, my wit sparked of amber and sapphire. Monica's smoldered like a windblown matchstick. I shared a subtle grin of satisfaction on my way out the door to the hallway.

Had my daddy lived he would have spoiled me the same as Monica's daddy, probably even more. I missed our old house. I missed the hidden corners and secret places I'd disappear to when I yearned for privacy. I missed the peach tree that sprawled across our front lawn. It stood so tall that in full summer, I could reach outside my bedroom window and grab a peach right from the branch.

After Mama ran out of Daddy's insurance money, we had no choice but to leave our beautiful home and move to Woodlane Trailer Park, the other side of Landon. It was painful for everyone. Becoming the only male in the house and changing schools hurt Luke even more. Luke wanted to escape from school, but I saw school as an escape. I was lucky to remain in the same high school. Even though Monica graced the hallways of Landon High, I refused to let her ruin my only happiness. School helped me in many ways. Not only because I loved to learn, but because of Mattéo Santoro.

CHAPTER 3

A rare find in Landon, Georgia, Mattéo Santoro's curly black hair and olive skin thrust my heart into a frenzy. Yankees rarely settled in Landon. Matt's New York City accent reminded me of Daddy. Born and raised in Brooklyn, Daddy spoke like a New Yorker until his dying day. Maybe Matt's unique dialect and infinite night-sky eyes attracted me to him the way Mama was drawn to Daddy. Fortunately, Matt was totally into me.

After homeroom, I rushed to my locker, hung up my coat, and grabbed my books. Matt caught my eye as he swaggered down the hallway in his tight black t-shirt, blue jeans and hi-top sneakers. Knees slightly bent as if he just hopped off of a horse, both hands buried deep inside his pockets, he had *cool* written all over him.

"Yo, *O-Liveuh!* C'mere," he said, using his eyes as a lasso.

I slammed my locker door shut, brushed my bangs to the side of my face, and smiled. Mama said a girl blessed with good teeth shouldn't waste a smile. Though she lacked a fine set of pearly whites, she used her other assets to her advantage.

Like the time she was caught speeding.

"Take note, girls," she said as she hiked up her skirt just above the knee and tilted her heart-shaped face toward the officer.

"What's the hurry, ma'am?" he said.

"I'm sorry, Officer, I didn't mean to be going so fast. I'll be sure to slow down."

Mama fluttered her lashes like two butterflies grazing a field of lilies. Feeling embarrassed as Mama capitalized on her sexual qualities, I sank down into the bottom of my seat; however, I did take note that she never did get that speeding ticket.

"Hey, Matt," I said. "What's goin' on?"

"I got tickets!" He pulled one hand from his pocket and waved two tickets in the air.

"Tickets for what?"

"For the Battle of the North and South Rock Show in Atlanta."

"Get out. You're teasing me."

"I'm not teasing." He held the tickets in front of my face.

I reached for them. "Let me see."

He hid them behind his back, coaxing me to wrap my arms around his waist, and I leaned into him. I whispered in his ear. "And who are you taking to that show?" Being only an inch or so shorter, I grabbed the tickets from his hand.

"I'm taking you, dummy." Matt swung his arm around my neck and pecked my cheek.

"Woo-hoo!" I danced around, waving the tickets in the air. "When is it?"

"Saturday. And my parents are going away for the weekend." He grinned. "We can go back to my house afterwards."

"O . . . kay," I said, but my excitement was also mixed with anxiety even though Matt had my heart wrapped around his finger.

The bell rang. I handed the tickets back to Matt. "Gotta go, see ya later." I hurried off.

I knew the plans he had in mind, and even though I'd imagined them over and over again, I wasn't sure if I was ready. Not even sure if I really wanted to go that far with Matt, but I was definitely curious.

My last boyfriend made a few attempts. However, each

time he did, the fear of his mama walking in on us would force his six-foot-frame off me. Actually, she saved me from suffocating. I wasn't exactly having a good time, but I knew it would not be like that with Matt; at least I hoped it wouldn't. In my fantasies, Matt would take me in his arms in the same romatic style that the lovers in the soap operas I watched did with one another.

Most girls in our school had already done it. Even though I came close, I was still afraid. Mama said, "First time you do it, it hurts more than it feels good. You'd better make sure it's with your husband, 'cause nobody else will have the patience to stick around after your screams ruin their moment of pleasure." I figured she just said that so I'd remain a virgin. Though I found it hard to believe she had been one before she married Daddy.

"Oh stop," CeCe hollered when she heard Mama and me talking. She hated when we spoke about sexual issues. It was like the whole subject grossed her out. I wondered about that sometimes.

During one of Jonzetta Davies' overnight parties, a bunch of girls talked about who had and hadn't done it. Jonzie said, "I got drunk the first time, didn't feel a thing."

"Same for me," Jonzie's cousin said.

Just like CeCe, Bessa Watson left the room that night, her

typical reaction when our discussions turned toward sex. On her way out, she left us with a message from her granny. "My granny told me sex out of wedlock is the worst thing you could do to ruin a marriage!"

Although Jonzie and Bessa were my best friends, listening to the both of them was like viewing life through a pair of bifocals. Jonzie was nearsighted, Bessa, farsighted. The two made me dizzy, yet somehow balanced.

After class, the day Matt showed me the tickets, I went to the cafeteria and joined the lunch line. Jonzie snuck up behind me and wrapped her hand over my eyes, "Guess who."

I spotted her immediately through the open gap between her ring finger and pinky. Not to mention her voice was most annoying. Originally raised in Arkansas, Jonzie's southern drawl sounded close to a foreign language, making it harder for me to detach myself from my own.

Always stepping in my personal space, her freckled ankle, which exposed a tattoo of a small candle burning at both ends, appeared beside mine. Her pants were rolled up just enough to see the bottom flame. The candle symbolized Jonzie and her twin brother, Michael, who died of leukemia in eighth grade. Like most twins, she and Mike were as close as a pair of skates. Before he died, he told Jonzie to keep the fire burning. I guess she took him close to literal.

"I forgot my lunch money," she whispered to me. "Can you lend me some?"

"*Me*, lend you money?" I said. "Huh, that's a joke. I only got enough money to toss in a fountain or buy an ice cream sandwich. I'll split an ice cream with you."

"Sure. Who needs the extra calories anyway."

Bessa strolled over with her perfect posture and a salad on her tray. She sat down across from me. "You have plans for the weekend?"

"Matt got tickets for the Battle of the North and South Rock Show in Atlanta," I replied, licking ice cream from my fingers. "We're going back to his house afterward. His parents are going away for the weekend." I grinned sheepishly.

Bessa raised her left eyebrow higher than it already sat on her forehead and placed the palm of her hand under her creamy white, zit-free chin. "If you go back to his house, you know *it's* gonna happen. Don'cha?"

"I haven't decided on that, yet." I took another bite from my ice cream and cocked my head to the side preparing to listen to a speech from Mother Theresa, a.k.a. Bessa. We'd been friends since the first grade. She lives with her granny, who used to be my Sunday school teacher. I had fond memories from those days, especially singing hymns. I remember once raising my hand after a song, asking, "How can God's hands be so big they can carry the whole world?"

Bessa's granny answered, "They're so big you can't see them. Kind of like the ocean caring for the sea creatures—even the ones buried deep near the ocean floor—the ones too afraid to reveal themselves to the light of day."

I thought of Mama, and how she revealed herself a little more than I would have liked. All the same, she was my Mama and God held her in her in his hands, and I needed to participate in His spiritual ecosystem. Regardless how much she made me want to crawl under a rock.

As far as Bessa . . . with constant reminders of moral values from her granny, I don't think Johnny Depp could've persuaded her into bed, and she was crazy mad for him.

Bessa continued with her speech. "I've told you before. If you do it before you get married it'll ruin your wedding night, and the rest of your marriage will be tarnished!"

I giggled. "If you don't stop wearing those baggy jumpsuits and talking like an old spinster, you'll never know 'cause you'll never find a husband."

"No! No! No!" Jonzie interrupted. "If you *don't* do it before you get married it'll ruin your wedding night."

Bessa's hand slipped from beneath her chin. "That makes no sense."

Jonzie leaned forward. "Listen up. Would you want to go waterskiing with someone who never water-skied?"

"Huh?" I looked at her like she had two skis on her head. "What in the world does that have to do with anything?"

"Remember the first time we went skiing with my cousin Hank?"

"Yeah."

"Remember how good he was, and how miserable we made him because we couldn't get up on those skis?"

"Yeah." I began picking at the mascara on my eyelashes, watching the flakes fall to the cafeteria table. I blew them off.

"Hank didn't have any fun that day. He spent the whole day turning the boat around and setting us up on the skis over and over again."

"Yeah," I said, impatiently, wondering where she was going with this?

"It's the same thing with sex," Jonzie said.

"Hush," Bessa whispered. The mere word threw her into a state of fear.

Jonzie rolled her eyes, cupped her mouth with her hands, and lowered her voice. "If a guy spends his wedding night trying get you up on skis the whole time and you fall off, it's gonna ruin the entire night. However, if you come as a skilled skier you'll glide across the lake of love in harmony."

Bessa placed the back of her right hand against her forehead like she felt faint. "Glide across the lake of love in harmony! What ancient romance novels have you been reading?" She folded her hands, set them on the table, stared deep into Jonzie's eyes and shook her head. "Your virginity is a gift you give to your husband on your wedding night. He'll hold you in the highest esteem if you save it for him. If you give it away before you get married you'll have nothing to give him, and he'll always wonder *who* got *his* wedding gift."

"You've been living with your Granny for way too long," Jonzie tossed her hand in the air as to swat a fly. She turned toward me again. "Olivia, listen to someone who knows. The first time is *not* fun, but it's *got* to be done so you can *get* to the fun. Ha! I rhymed." She held her chin high, stole an olive from Bessa's plate, and popped it into her mouth.

I guess Mama was telling the truth on that one. But I didn't share much of what Mama said, even with Bessa, who knew Daddy before he died. After we moved to Woodlane, I stopped having friends inside my home, so they rarely saw her anyway. Bessa was too proper to say anything negative about Mama, and only asked about her occasionally. Jonzie already knew Mama was slightly unusual, and left it at that.

* * *

After school, I hopped the front steps and let myself inside. CeCe and Luke weren't home yet. I grabbed a bottle of Coke from the refrigerator, propped my feet up and put my drink down on the coffee table. I dug the remote out from in between the cushions, turned on MTV and watched a Queen video. When it was over, I clicked on the channels then stopped at an afternoon talk show. The host had white hair and huge eye glasses. He was talking with a psychiatrist.

The doctor sat in a chair across from him. They talked about things that sounded like Mama. I took my feet off the coffee table, leaned toward the TV, and listened. First, the doctor used the word *mania*. He said it caused high levels of energy and sleeplessness. *That's Mama,* I thought. It was like every so often, someone plugged her in and recharged her battery.

Then he said *schizophrenia,* which can include hallucinations. That sounded like Mama, too. *So maybe she was hallucinating when she buried the turkey. Not to mention the time she went on about seeing Daddy in the meat department at Kroegers.*

Lack of emotion.

Sometimes I felt as if Mama didn't feel anything at all.

Disorganized thoughts, difficulty concentrating, mania, depression, schizophrenia . . . everything the doctor said sounded like Mama.

Just as the doctor on the television was about to give a phone number to call for help, I heard sounds from the bedroom. I didn't see Mama or CeCe's car, and Luke was still at school. My heart pounded and panic clamped down on my throat. I grabbed the cordless phone and dialed 911. I whispered for the Landon Police Department.

"Emergency, can I help you?" A female voice said.

"I think someone's in my house."

"Where do you live, ma'am?"

"Three Stargazer Court, Woodlane Trailer Park . . . in Landon."

"We'll send someone right out."

I hung up, ran outside, and hid behind a car parked across the street where I could see the front and back door of the trailer. Why would someone want to rob my house? I wondered, panting from fear. The big houses were across the main highway, over where Monica Bradshaw lived. Maybe the thief was lost or desperate.

All of the sudden, the back door opened and an elderly man

with disheveled silver and black hair placed his foot on the top stair. He looked more like a salesman than a thief, dressed in a dark gray suit with a white wrinkled shirt. His tie hung out of his top pocket and his hands were empty.

He could still be a thief, I told myself. *Maybe he took Mama's jewelry*—the jewelry Daddy gave her. *Maybe he hid it in the pocket with his tie.* That was about the only thing of value we had except for the TV and VCR player.

He stepped onto the patio at the same instant the police pulled up.

"Stop right there!" the officer demanded.

The man held his hands up. "What'd I do, what'd I do?"

"Do you have identification?" The officer asked.

The man opened his suit jacket and went for his wallet. The police officer raised his gun and shouted, "Keep your hands up!"

The Venetian blinds on Miss Ruth's kitchen window cracked open. I saw both her and Bubbles Clayton's beady eyes peeking through. Next door to her, the silhouette of a mother holding a baby appeared behind a pair of sheer curtains. Others blatantly stepped outside onto their patios, and their gaping eyes held our trailer hostage while they whispered to one another.

I stood behind the car, frozen, waiting for the ordeal to end, when the trailer's front door suddenly opened and Mama

36

appeared on the patio, her hair messy and dress wrinkled.

Mama was in there with him?

I wanted to stay hidden, not from what I thought was a burglar, but from everyone who stood staring at my mama with their pernicious thoughts. Instead, I bolted across the street to the trailer.

CHAPTER 4

Mama stepped onto the patio. I rushed to her side and grabbed her by the shoulders. "Mama, are you all right? Did that man hurt you?" I felt myself start to shake.

"It's okay darlin', he's just a friend." Her mauve lipstick shadowed her upper lip.

She gently pushed my hands away and strolled up to the police officer and whispered in his ear. He nodded, tipped his hat and left. Then she walked over to the stranger and kissed his cheek. He slipped into the powder blue Cadillac parked behind the trailer, where I never saw it when I came home from school. I suddenly realized what I feared had gone on actually had, and the thought of Mama in that way made me ill.

"Who was that man?" I demanded.

"His name is Westin." Mama tilted her head and waved

goodbye as he pulled away. "He gave me a ride home."

"Why'd you need a ride home? Where's your car?"

Mama smoothed her dress. "I misplaced it."

"You what?"

She lifted her hands from her dress and threw them in the air matter-of-factly, and sauntered inside the house. "You heard me, Olivia."

"You misplace your slippers or your keys, not your *car!* You're telling me you got in the car with a stranger?"

"He's not a stranger, now." She grinned.

"He could have hurt you," I said. Our roles had completely reversed I was acting as if I were the mother and she the child. "You've told us a ton of times never to get into a car with a stranger, and you go and do it yourself. Mama, I just don't understand you." I shook my head.

She stared into space as if nothing had happened. I figured it was in her character when she had hiked her skirt up for the policeman, but that paled in comparison to what she'd done this time. My fears about her were confirmed.

"Olivia, bring me some sweet tea," she said.

"Yes, Ma'am." I stomped into the kitchen and flung the refrigerator door open, slammed a glass onto the counter, almost breaking it, and poured the sweet tea. It was obvious Mama needed to get to a doctor. She had more than quirks. Now, I believed more than ever, she had what the doctor on TV was talking about. Every symptom fit her. After I shared my findings with CeCe, she'd finally believe it too.

Mama finished her tea and lay down for a nap. I wondered if CeCe had put Sominex in the entire pitcher. Then I grabbed a phone book from the closet. No regular doctor could help Mama; she needed a specialist. That's what the man on the talk show said. I flipped through the pages until I found a listing of psychiatrists and wrote down some names and numbers. Most were in Atlanta, which was over an hour away from Landon.

CeCe finally came home. Tired from her day-cleaning job and going to school, her face said, "Don't tell me nothing." After she glimpsed at mine she asked, "What's the matter now?"

I told her what happened. She ripped the rubber band out of her hair and massaged her head with both hands. We had never gotten into a serious conversation about Mama's behavior before. We just dealt with the situations as they came along. I knew CeCe had always known something was seriously wrong. Maybe she thought if she ignored it, it would go away. I thought that many times, too. But it wasn't going away. It was coming back more often and stronger than ever before.

"Let me see the list of doctors," CeCe said. She attempted

to read the first name aloud. "Dr. Jsnr . . . nope. I'm not taking Mama to a doctor whose name I can't even pronounce."

I should have known she'd give me a hard time. "It's not like there's a whole bunch of psychological specialists in Landon," I said.

"How 'bout this one?" She circled another name and handed me the paper.

"Dr. Smith." I raised my eyebrows. "He's all the way in Atlanta. Your car will never make it."

"We'll take Mama's car."

"Uh . . . speaking of Mama's car. There's something I forgot to tell you."

* * *

"I'll do the talking," CeCe said, and moved ahead of me into the police station.

"Whatever you say." I pretended to zip my lips.

She approached the counter and waved to the clerk sitting behind a desk. "Pardon me, Ma'am, but I'd like to retrieve my mother's automobile. I called earlier, and someone informed me it's been impounded."

A woman leaned over the counter, wearing a pair of cat-eyed shaped glasses like something you'd see in an old movie. The top button hole on her blouse stretched as if it were about to pop due to her wide neck. She peered down her nose at CeCe and me, and her magnified eyes took shape to the glasses.

"Do you have the bill of sale?" she asked.

"No, ma'am, we can't seem to find it," CeCe said.

"How about the registration?"

CeCe smiled gently. "The registration is in the car."

"Well, I can't let you inside the car without proof you own it."

"If you could just let us in the car we'll get the registration, and we'll show you. I believe it's in the glove compartment," CeCe said. Her voice becoming tense, and her face growing red.

"Sorry, can't do that."

My heart was beating so fast I couldn't keep myself quiet one second longer, and the invisible zipper on my lips split open. I stepped in front of CeCe and stuck my face directly in front of the clerk.

"Maybe you could just open the darn car and take the registration out yourself, then?"

CeCe elbowed me and whispered, "Shut. Up." She turned a beaming smile toward the clerk. "Ma'am, our mother is sick. She's unable to tell us where the bill of sale is. We only have the registration, which is in the car. I have the key." She dangled it in front of the clerk's face. "Can you please make an exception?"

She opened her wallet and pointed. "The address on my license matches the registration to the car. If you can just get it, you'll see."

"No, ma'am, them's the rules," she said, as if she enjoyed denying our request. It didn't make sense to me how this woman could be so mean for the mere pleasure of it. All she had to say was *yes*, and our problem would be solved.

I took a deep breath so I would speak and not yell, but something in between came out. "This is ridiculous! Why can't you give us a break?"

"I'm sorry, but when you come back with the bill of sale or the registration I will be happy to release your mother's car."

I couldn't imagine this woman being happy about anything except keeping us from the one thing we needed. My face felt flushed and my thoughts spewed into words. "How are we supposed to get that document when IT'S IN THE DAMN CAR?"

She slapped a form onto the counter. "Fill this out and send it to the address listed. And by the way, you will be charged twenty dollars per day as long as your car remains in the impound yard," she said, spitting the "p" in "impound" into tiny droplets onto the form.

I pointed my finger in front of the clerk's face. "This is just wrong! I want to speak to someone else."

The woman smirked, and said, "There is no one else," and directed her attention to the lady behind us.

All heated, I wanted to share a few more of my thoughts with her, but I had enough smarts to know it wouldn't make a difference. CeCe nudged me along and we strutted away.

"I can't believe that witch." I murmured. "What are we gonna do now?"

"Don't worry," CeCe answered. Her voice calm. "I've got a plan."

* * *

Luke was smart and CeCe resourceful, a combination that often worked to our advantage. As soon as we returned home, CeCe snuck inside the house while Mama napped and motioned for Luke to come out.

"What's goin' on?" he asked, but his eyes were already beaming.

Luke loved when CeCe and I included him in our schemes, because we usually asked him to do something he shouldn't be doing. Like the time CeCe had him sit outside the grocery store wearing his baseball cap while he held a can pretending he was fundraising. Mama had lost her purse that week, and we didn't have any food in the house. Fortunately, Mama found her purse a few days later in the broom closet. The following week, CeCe secretly dropped the same amount of money Luke raised from *his* fundraiser into the can of the real one to make up for what we'd done.

"Mama's car's been impounded," CeCe told him. "And I need you to hop the fence at the impound yard and get her car registration out of the glove compartment."

"Why?"

"They won't give the car back unless we have the registration," I said. "And they won't let us into the car to get it. And until we get it, they're charging us twenty dollars a day."

Luke understood the value of money more than most boys his age because of all we'd gone through after Daddy died.

"Twenty bucks!" His eyes bulged out as if it were his own money. "Dang. Sure, I'll do it," he said. "When do we go?"

Mama rarely paid attention to our whereabouts, but we didn't want to make it too obvious us leaving all at once. After sundown, one by one, we disappeared out the door and piled into CeCe's '77 Impala. We arrived at the impound yard and Luke hopped the fence and returned a few minutes later. Everything seemed to go as planned; except Luke returned empty-handed.

"Where's the registration?" CeCe asked.

"The only thing in the glove compartment was a spoiled

sandwich," he said, climbing into the Impala's back seat. "I almost blew chunks from the stink. I didn't find anything else, except a bunch of crumpled papers. I left the windows open so the smell would let out."

"Now what are we gonna do?" I said to CeCe, tired and sorry she carried Mama's burdens, but always in the back of my mind, fearful they would soon be mine.

"Let's go," she said and drove away.

"Where we going?" Luke asked.

"Yeah, where we going?"

CeCe didn't answer. I squinted at her in the darkened car, trying to guess what was going on in her head. Her eyes; two hard stones bleeding confusion. I heeded to her stare and didn't speak.

We drove back to Woodlane, and she pulled the car over. "Get out."

I followed her command. Luke followed me. Once we were all out, CeCe began pacing in the street. Since she wouldn't talk and neither Luke nor I knew what to do or say, we leaned against the car and waited. I counted twenty-four paces before she stopped and faced Luke.

"Our only choice is to take back the car ourselves," she said.

Luke's eyes smiled. I could almost see twinkling stars floating out. "You mean you want me to steal Mama's car?"

"It's not really stealing," she said, then inhaled and held her breath for an instant. "It's just taking back what's ours."

She placed her hands on Luke's shoulders and stared him square in the eyes. "Listen, Luke, you can't do anything like this again. These are unusual circumstances requiring unusual means. And don't tell a soul. Got it? And when you start the car, drive *slowly* and *directly home*. I mean it, Luke. Got it?"

He nodded. "Go home and don't tell a soul." Then, he gazed up at CeCe with puppy dog eyes and said, "Not a one?"

CeCe's eyes narrowed. No doubt her mind was racing. Luke did an about-face and got into the car. A risky plan, but we didn't know what else to do or where to turn.

CHAPTER 5

Involved with her nighttime TV show, Mama stared at the television willing her characters to do what she'd expected of them. No one could break her trance. No one tried. We each left the room one at a time, just like before. Once outside, we hopped back into CeCe's car. I sat in the back seat and Luke in the front. His right leg bounced at a quicker speed than usual. My armpits dripped with sweat. CeCe pulled a rubber band from the front pocket of her Levi shorts and wrapped her hair in a ponytail.

"Wait, we should pray," she said.

"*Pray?* You want us to pray that God helps us steal Mama's car? Maybe Mama's not the only kooky one around here," I said.

CeCe glared at me, then closed her eyes and prayed

silently. When she finished, we drove back to the impound yard. It seemed darker than before. She handed Luke a flashlight and the keys, and he hopped the fence and stirred off into the night, again. While we waited, my stomach acid made sounds like it was eating my organs.

And then, I had an urge that was the last thing I wanted. And the urge just kept getting stronger. "Uh, CeCe," I said. "I've got to go to the bathroom."

"Hold it."

I crossed my legs. "Don't you think I'm trying?"

"Go behind that bush." She pointed out the window of the car toward a dark corner.

I shot her a desperate look. "I don't have any tissues."

"I knew I should have left you home." She dug inside her pocketbook and handed me some napkins from Dunkin Donuts.

I tiptoed across the brush on the clay ground fearing I would come across a snake or rat, then pulled down my shorts and peed as quickly as possible, all the while smacking the mosquitoes flicking against my bare legs.

Just moments after I got back into the car, we heard the sound of an engine coming through the darkness. We held our breath, wondering if we were about to be caught.

Thankfully, it was Luke. Mama's car pulled up and stopped

just inside the gate. We watched as he jumped out of the driver's side door and climbed the gate and went for the padlock. Fortunately, a boy he had met when we first moved to Woodlane taught him how to pick a lock. When he came home bragging about it, CeCe was mortified.

Mama only said, "Maybe Luke will grow up to be a locksmith." How could we have known the skill he learned back then would be so handy now?

A moment later, CeCe and I heard a click through our open windows and saw him push the gate open, then quickly get back inside Mama's car. He pulled away and sped down the road. Which was exactly what CeCe told him not to do. We followed, seeing him weave in and out of traffic, running two stops signs and almost up a curb.

"What the heck is he *doing?*" CeCe shouted.

She tried to catch up to him. My sandals flew off. I pushed my feet hard against the floor and grabbed onto the sides of the bucket seat. My fingers felt purple, my heels blue.

"He's gonna get us caught," I said. "We're definitely going to jail!"

"Shut up, Olivia, I need to concentrate" she said, and peeled around the corner to keep up.

My heart raced and gurgled. I could barely breathe. Clearly,

CeCe had the right idea about praying. Luke pulled into the trailer park too fast and jammed on the brakes, nearly colliding with the picket fence in front of our trailer. He flung the car door open and jumped outside before CeCe had a chance to open her door.

"AAAAH," he screamed, then, "AAAAH! AAAAH!"

"What's the matter?" CeCe and I hollered in a loud whisper, fearing that someone in the trailer park would hear.

"There's critters in the car!"

"Critters?" I stepped back and squinted in the dark, just in time to see a family of junkyard cats tumble out behind him and scatter into the woods.

"I shouldn't have left the windows open," he said, breathing heavy.

"Luke, is that you?" Mama stepped onto the patio. "Watcha all doin' outside in the dark— Oh, look! Somebody brought my car back. It must've been that nice man I met the other day. Westin." Mama smiled. "Y'all come on inside and watch *TV* with me." She waved us in and we followed like zombies.

Just as we sat down and my heart stopped beating hard enough to break through my chest, the telephone rang. CeCe jumped up and yanked it off the hook. "Hello."

It's the police, I thought as the bitter taste of acid re-visited my throat. *They discovered us and they're coming to get us!*

Luke and I stared at CeCe, trying to hear, but the TV was too loud. She nodded a few times, but we couldn't tell what was going on. Then, she hung up.

"Wrong number." CeCe closed her eyes, stretched her arms behind her head, and let out a longwinded sigh.

I let out ten.

No one ever did come knocking on our door. So many cars filled the impound yard, they must not have noticed Mama's car missing. However, after that, Luke took a liking to stealing, and CeCe felt as if it was all her fault. Right then I knew I'd have to find a way to straighten Luke out so CeCe wouldn't feel so pressured. It might make her want to leave all the more. But it, and anything else, would have to wait until after the concert.

CHAPTER 6

"I want big hair, big as Dolly Parton, but a cooler version." I told Jonzie's aunt, who owned a hairdressing shop she operated out of her garage. "I'm going to a concert and I need to look drop-dead gorgeous."

"You need a wig to get hair as big as Dolly's, Honey," her aunt replied. "Besides, you're much too tiny for hair like that. It'll knock you off balance. How 'bout something in between and more . . . contemporary?"

"But Dolly's small," I argued, and people everywhere still loved her.

She placed her hands on her hips. "Dolly's a famous country singer, and even though you've got a pretty good package for someone your size, Dolly has a whole post office."

"O . . . kay, but make it wild," I said, and sat back in the chair and let her do her thing.

When she finished, I had big hair. I had big, hard, shiny hair. I had big, hard, shiny, *ugly* hair. I couldn't complain; I'd gotten exactly what I'd asked for. Thank goodness Jonzie's aunt didn't charge me. I would have died if I paid for a hairdo like that. I must have grabbed a bunch of antique magazines when I came up with the crazy idea to ask for big hair. And everyone on Main Street in Landon must have thought so too.

Cars beeped their horns at me while I walked back home. Old ladies whispered. Little kids pointed and laughed. I pulled my sunglasses from my purse and slapped them on so no one could see the tears in my eyes. I wanted so badly for everything to be perfect for Matt. No worries, no burdens, no Mama. I just wanted to be sixteen and have fun.

Wide-eyed, CeCe took one look at the sight of me and said, "What the heck happened to you?"

"I got big hair."

She wrapped her hands around her stomach, bent over, and started cracking up.

If the upcoming night wasn't so important to me, I would have probably been laughing along with CeCe. Instead, I wanted to cry. But I didn't need puffy eyes to go along with my puffy head, which resembled a dirty beige lampshade de-threading at the edges.

After CeCe finished her laugh-fest, she said, "Wash it out. I just saw one of those makeover shows. I'll redo it for you."

CeCe transformed me from a garage sale bargain to a hot babe. Like Jonzie's aunt said, big hair wasn't meant for my head.

Matt was picking me up at 6:30, which gave me just enough time to run back to the bathtub and shave my legs. I still hadn't decided whether to go forth with his plan, but I wanted to be ready just in case.

"Have fun," CeCe said, and took off in her car mysteriously like usual.

At 6:45, Matt pulled up in his black mustang and honked the horn. Like always, Miss Ruth scoped the neighborhood from her patio. If I hadn't seen her wrinkly claw pop up every so often holding the new hand mirror she used to view the sights behind her, I might have thought she was dead.

I opened the back door and held my finger up to Matt. "Just one more minute!"

His dimples sunk into his cheeks as he shot me a smile.

I checked the mirror one last time. My black jeans looked great with CeCe's hot pink blouse. She would have killed me if she caught me wearing it. But she got new clothes all the time since she had a job. I was sick of the same old outfits. *If I lose five pounds, I'll be able to borrow her pants too*, I thought while I turned and glanced at my bubble-butt. Then I grabbed a bottle of her perfume and sprayed my neck.

"Bye, Mama. I'll be home later," I said.

She was staring at the TV so hard, she didn't notice me. With Luke and CeCe gone, I felt nervous about leaving her alone. The television had become her best friend. She talked to it more than she ever had before. It seemed like the TV characters had a direct line to her brain. They were her family and we were the commercials.

I left the house and got into Matt's car. He leaned over and kissed me. His sweet smell filled the air. I breathed him in and put Mama out of my mind.

"Hey, Babe," he said. His black velvet eyes lusted after me; his tongue grazed his bottom lip. I realized the pockets on CeCe's pink blouse brought attention to my chest. Not my intention. My gut told me it would *not* be easy to say *no* to Matt Santoro.

* * *

Scantily dressed girls and rock 'n roll wannabies wrapped around the building leading up to the entrance of the concert hall. From time to time I caught Matt's eyes scanning the flow of females. I tried to hide my insecurity. Stares from girls wearing scads of makeup and cool clothes made me wonder if they were checking out Matt or me. Maybe they were wondering what someone like him was doing with someone like me. Even with the hair makeover, I didn't feel I could compete with them.

Matt had hidden a bottle of vodka mixed with lemonade inside his leather jacket. I'd never drank more than two beers before and this would be a first, but since the girls at Jonzie's sleepover who'd done *it* said they were drunk at the time, I figured that's what I would be.

Once we got inside, Matt offered me some of his concoction. I wasn't fond of the taste, but I enjoyed the warm, tingly sensation that enveloped me a short while later. My blood ran hot through every one of my veins. Right then I understood why sex took place so often when a person drank liquor. I suddenly wanted Matt's hands all over me.

The warm-up band played, and people shouted for the main act. The guys in the crowd shook their fists in the air to the drummer's beat, and the girls shook their butts. The lead singer of the main act strutted on stage doing both. The crowd roared. After many sips from Matt's bottle, I danced too in the smoke-filled, sweat-smelling arena.

After the concert, we arrived at Matt's front door and

tripped up the steps. I gazed around and realized Matt's house was bigger than ten trailers put together. Most boys from this part of town stopped asking me out after I moved to Woodlane, but Matt was different. Coming from the great melting pot of New York City, he grew up among people from all backgrounds. He didn't care where I lived.

He fiddled with the house key while I stroked his curly hair. I giggled, but noticed his breathing was a lot heavier than before. He opened the door and we fell inside, landing on the couch, Matt on top of me. His warm and wet tongue darted back and forth inside my mouth.

We kissed for a while, then his hands began roaming . . . stopping . . . roaming, and then hurried. I felt hot, dizzy, hesitant. I sat up. Matt began kissing my neck and unbuttoning my blouse. I think I wanted to stop him but my hands wouldn't move. I thought about what Jonzie said. *"The first time is not fun, but it's got to be done."*

Then Bessa's words flew into my mind. *"No! No! No!"*

After Matt removed my blouse, he pulled his t-shirt off and began kissing me again. Our skin melted together. I held him tight and kissed him until the room began to spin. I couldn't speak. He stood up and dropped his pants to the floor. The room spun faster, and the contents of my stomach projected onto the carpet and all over his pants. I don't know whether it was the liquor or the sight of Matt standing naked in front of me, but I did know I wanted to die.

CHAPTER 7

After apologizing to Matt and helping him clean up the mess, he drove me home. Half disappointed we hadn't done it, and half relieved, I said goodbye without giving him a goodnight kiss for fear he'd smell my sickly breath. I tiptoed up the steps to the back door of the trailer so Mama wouldn't hear me. Not that it would've really mattered, unless she felt like talking, then I'd be trapped. Trapped again. I opened the door slowly, crept into the darkness . . . and tripped over CeCe, who was asleep on the floor.

"What the heck are you doing?" I asked.

"Mama's taken off twice around the neighborhood in her nightgown. Luke is sleeping on the floor by the *front* door. We've got to keep her inside. She'll end up on the highway. It's like she's sleepwalking or something." CeCe pulled the blanket up to her chin. "You stink. Were you drinking?"

"Yeah," I said and covered my mouth, feeling another wave of nausea.

"Go brush your teeth," she whispered. "And take my blouse off this instant and go to sleep. You might have floor duty tomorrow night."

It was too much to take. First Matt, now Mama. I wanted to wake up tomorrow and find it had all been a dream. I hated the trailer, I hated what Mama had become, and I hated feeling so alone. While I lay in bed picking off my mascara, a million thoughts ran through my head. The television show about mental illness was one of them. Now that we had Mama's car back, and the concert was over, we had to get her to the doctor in Atlanta.

The next morning my head throbbed even harder and my mouth was incredibly dry. I washed my face, brushed my teeth, and downed a glass of water. Thinking maybe a few crackers would make me feel better, I made my way to the kitchen and found CeCe still asleep in front of the back door. But Luke had left his position and I didn't see him anywhere.

Mama neither.

"CeCe! She's gone," I shouted. "Mama's gone! Luke's gone too!"

She jumped up, bleary-eyed and confused. "What are you

talking about?"

"Luke isn't by the front door, or anywhere in the house. I don't know if they're together or if Luke just left the house and Mama took off."

CeCe opened the front door to see if Mama's car was there; it was. This frightened me even more.

"Get dressed," she said.

While CeCe quickly put on her shoes, I pulled on a pair of jeans and slipped on my sneakers and we bolted out the front door. We scoured the trailer park by foot. We realized she could be in someone's house, trailing the highway, or even worse.

Just as we were about to jump in CeCe's car, Luke showed up on his bicycle.

"Where've you been?" CeCe barked.

He flicked his kickstand down and stood for a moment, then ran his fingers through his scraggly shoulder length hair. "I was starving, so I went to get a doughnut." He held out a bag. "I got some for you too."

My stomach clenched. "Mama's gone!"

"Sorry," he said, voice crackling. "She was sleeping when I left. I tried to hurry."

He began blinking his eyes uncontrollably, refusing to cry. CeCe's eyes darted back and forth, the way they did when she was thinking hard. I felt too hung-over to think at all.

"Come on," she said after a moment. "We've gotta find her."

We drove up and down the highway. I searched the left side of the road and Luke scanned the right.

"There's no way she would've made it this far," CeCe said after a while. "Let's go back."

My stomach rumbled, and I thought I would be sick again. Not so much because of the hangover, but because of my fear. Guilt began attacking me as well. If I had not gone to the concert, we might have been able to get Mama to the doctor sooner and she would not have disappeared.

"I'm gonna call Grandma," CeCe said. "It probably won't make a difference, but I don't know what else to do. We can't call the police. They wouldn't understand. She hasn't been gone long enough for them to consider her missing."

She grabbed the phone, dialed Grandma, and handed me the receiver. "Here, you talk to her. She likes you better."

"Why do you think she likes me better?"

CeCe shrugged. "Just talk to her."

Grandma picked up on the first ring.

"Hi, Grandma. It's, uh . . . Olivia. . . . No, things aren't too good. Mama hasn't been acting right lately, and now we can't find her. We don't know what to do. We've checked everywhere! No, Grandma, I think it's more serious. Okay, I will. Bye."

"What the heck did she say?" CeCe asked.

I slammed the phone down. She said, "Oh, don't worry, child. Your mama loves to take long walks. I remember one time she was gone an entire night. We got a little worried, but she came home and told us she fell asleep beneath a beautiful weeping willow tree."

A weeping willow tree—no wonder Daddy never liked Grandma.

I kicked the kitchen chair and shouted, "Grandma said she was on her way to the Senior Center and we should call back when Mama comes home. Yeah, if she does come home."

I closed my eyes and massaged my temples. "She doesn't care. She doesn't get it," I said, and my head throbbed even harder.

CeCe finally let her tears fall, and that scared me almost worse than Mama being gone. My sister didn't cry often. If she had no idea what we should do, who would? Luke just sat zoned out on the TV. I sat down in Mama's chair and rocked back and forth; and we waited.

* * *

The one thing you can count on in Georgia, winter or summer, is a thunderstorm when that's the last thing you want. By 2:00 p.m., the sky darkened and it began to rain. Thinking of Mama lost out in the rain caused my heart to ache even more. I stepped onto the patio, and felt the temperature had dropped. A lot. I didn't know if she even had her sweater.

Finally, CeCe called the police.

I couldn't tell what the officer was saying to her, but the lump in my throat grew each second she stayed on the phone. When she hung up, she said, "The police told me they'd received a call earlier about a woman wandering down the highway."

"Mama?" Luke blurted, keeping his eyes on the TV.

"I don't know. But they said the caller told them the woman seemed . . . disoriented. When they checked, she had vanished. They said they'd keep an eye out for her and call us if they find her."

She turned to Luke and said, "Stay here, just in case Mama comes back. We're gonna take another look around."

He nodded without turning his head to her.

When we got back, Luke had fallen asleep on the couch. CeCe threw a blanket over him then lay down on the other couch. I found some pillows and a blanket and put them on the floor. We all slept in the too-small living room that night. That's where Mama spent most of her time. When she came back, this is where she would come first. *If* she came back. Even so, sleeping there made me, and probably all three of us, feel closer to her, and closer to each other.

* * *

That was Sunday. Monday arrived and Luke and I didn't go to school, and CeCe didn't go to work or school.

"I better call Mama's boss," CeCe said.

"What are you gonna say to him?" I asked, wondering if she'd tell him the truth.

"I'll say she's got the flu and that she'll be out for a few days . . . just in case she needs some extra time to rest after we find her." She grabbed the telephone and punched in Mama's work number. After she finished, she looked at Luke and me. "Maybe I should call your school, too Luke." She picked the phone back up.

I glanced out the window every so often, willing Mama to come walking down the street. She didn't.

While CeCe dialed Luke's school she said, "I'm not gonna call yours, Olivia. The school nurse will probably think I'm you, and that'll only cause problems. But you had better make sure you make up the work you miss. I don't want you falling behind."

As soon as she hung up with Luke's school, CeCe called her boss and said she'd be out for a few days as well.

CeCe and I barely ate anything. Wracking our brains trying to figure out where Mama could be, made it difficult to have an appetite, anyway. Luke, who could probably eat while in a coma, didn't have much food to choose from. Mama hadn't gone shopping in a while, and most of the food was rotted. She had left her purse at home, which made us more nervous. She never left the house without it. CeCe opened it, checking for money. A twenty-dollar bill stuck out of her wallet, and a few dollars in change lay at the bottom of the purse.

CeCe pulled out the twenty and handed it to Luke. "Go get something to eat," she said. "Don't spend it all. We need to conserve."

Luke shoved the money into his pocket and took off on his bike. Mama had been gone for two nights and two days. By now, I was picturing her lying in a creek at the bottom of the hill across the highway, a place we had checked, but she wasn't there. Sometimes, I pictured her held hostage inside someone's home, gagged and bound to a chair. Other times, I'd envision her lost in the woods, pinching leaves off trees and dropping them like breadcrumbs, leaving a trail for us to follow. Only she didn't realize her leaves fell among thousands already on the forest floor.

Each time one of these scenarios ran through my head, anger squeezed my insides 'til they hurt. Why couldn't we have grandparents who would rush to our side to help their widowed daughter? Or an aunt who did more than send a Christmas check once a year? Why couldn't just *one* member of our family live in Georgia? Why couldn't just one member of our family care?

"It's my fault."

I looked over at CeCe, who was holding Mama's purse like it was a baby. "What are you talking about?" I said.

She hung her head and shook it back and forth. "While you were out getting your hair done yesterday, I told her I thought she should go to the doctor. She said, 'What on the earth for?' I told her why, and she practically breathed fire at me. She didn't talk to me for the rest of the night."

"That explains why she looked so out of it when I left after you did. But that's not *your* fault. I'm the one who brought up the idea about her going to the doctor after watching that TV program."

"Yeah, but I should have been more gentle with her."

The front door swung open and Luke entered holding a bag filled with burgers and fries. We sat down at the kitchen table. I took a few bites, but it felt as if I were trying to eat live bugs.

CeCe just pushed her food around the plate, picking apart the burger without much of it disappearing. Luke ate our leftovers.

We had to find Mama. We had to help her. I wanted it all to stop. No doubt, CeCe did too, but she must have decided to distract us for a while. Or maybe she needed to distract herself. After Luke finished eating, she sat down on the living room chair and swung her legs over the arm.

"Remember our first winter here?" she asked. "When Mama sold her new car and bought that old Chevy because we needed the money to heat the trailer, and we missed the bus and Mama had to drive us to school?"

How could I forget that day? The car door wouldn't shut, so Mama handed us her scarf and told us to attach it to the door. We yanked on it every time the car turned a corner so no one would fall out."

"Yeah, yeah, I remember that." I smiled. "I remember Mama yelling, 'Hold on tight, I don't wanna lose none of ya!'"

We all had a good chuckle about that, then I said, "And oh, don't forget the holes in the floor under the carpet mats."

"Yeah, yeah, the holes," CeCe said. "Mama always feared we'd drop Luke through one of 'em."

Luke wrinkled his nose and scrunched his eyebrows. "Y'all wouldn't have thrown me out, would ya?"

CeCe and I laughed harder. "Heck, we tried to *keep* you from falling out. Every time we stopped for a red light, you tried your darnedest to escape."

"That's 'cause I wanted to be a stuntman." Luke smiled, showing all his teeth.

The three of us laughed like we hadn't a worry in the world. Life stood still, happily for a few moments, until the telephone rang. Still laughing, I grabbed it first.

"Hello?"

"This is the Henry County Police Department," said the voice on the other end.

CHAPTER 8

The emergency room at Henry Medical Center smelled like cigarette smoke and urine washed over with antiseptic. I'd never been there before, and I didn't expect to see so many people that resembled those with the symptoms the doctor on the talk show spoke about. Although most needed physical care, many seemed to need mental health care, and this wasn't a mental hospital.

Some of the people roamed about like zombies in B-movies. Their vacant stares said, "I'm still here, please come find me." Many of the patients were pacing, as if they were taking part in some kind of weird ritual. Some shouted words at random. One woman seemed to be speaking in a language only she could understand. I was afraid to make eye contact with anyone, for fear someone would approach me. But I knew I had to look around the room.

An old woman with only one-half of her head braided asked me for a cigarette. One already hung from her twisted lips. It felt like we wandered into a secret society meeting and we had better find Mama and get out while we could.

I overheard one of the nurses say to another, "It must be a full moon tonight."

"My goodness," the other nurse responded. "I haven't seen it like this in quite some time. That strong lunar force is drawing them out like vampires to a blood bank."

CeCe and I approached the desk. "Excuse me, Ma'am," CeCe said to the desk clerk. "The police told us a woman that fits our mother's description has been brought here."

"What's her name?"

"Cassandra Travis," I answered, surprised at how faint my voice sounded.

She thumbed through her roster. "The police brought in a Jane Doe. We've been asking her name, but she won't tell us." The clerk motioned toward a nurse. "They're here to see Jane Doe in room twelve."

The nurse nodded and said, "Follow me."

I thought of Luke and was glad we'd left him at home.

CeCe and I followed the nurse down a long corridor. Blue curtains covered doorways on each side. We approached the last room on the left, and the nurse pulled a chart from a hook on the wall. She opened the curtain. "This is Jane Doe."

"That's not Mama," I said, disappointed and glad at the same time. "This woman is black."

The nurse tilted her head and glanced at me sympathetically. "She's not black, Honey, she's dirty. She won't let us bathe her."

The woman lay flat on her stomach as if she were dead. The nurse patted her on the back. "Wake up, Ma'am."

CeCe and I moved in closer.

"It couldn't be," I whispered.

"Look." CeCe pointed at the triangular-shaped scar on the leg peeking out from beneath the blanket.

Mama had gotten one just like that from the engine of Daddy's motorcycle years ago. She told us how excited she was to go riding for the first time, but she'd been wearing shorts.

"The muffler got me good," she'd said. "I should've known better."

Now, it was the only way I could recognize her.

The nurse rolled her over. "Sit up, Ma'am. You have visitors."

She lifted her head so we could see her face. It *was* Mama. Her once-fair skin was almost as dark as her hair, filthy as a dirty rag on a garage floor. Her vacant eyes moved back and forth between CeCe and me.

"I don't know these people. Make them leave," she said, and looked away from us.

Tears streamed down my face. "Why's she saying she doesn't know us?" My voice cracked, but I didn't care. I reached out and clasped her hand. "Mama, it's us, Olivia and CeCe. We've come to take you home."

She pulled her hand away and didn't answer, just kept glaring at us like we were bugs on her shoe.

The nurse placed her arm on my shoulder. "Is this your first experience with your mama . . . like this?"

My bottom lip quivered. Words refused to escape my lips. I began picking off my mascara and two eyelashes fell into my hand. I peeled them apart and let them fall to the ground.

"Yes," CeCe answered. "She's been doing things. Things she wouldn't normally do. It's like she's on drugs . . . and I know my mama would never take drugs. Maybe someone else drugged her."

CeCe looked at the nurse for confirmation.

"I'm telling you, CeCe, her mind is sick," I blurted. "I saw it on TV."

The nurse cleared her throat and flipped through the medical chart. She looked down slightly, then glanced up and nodded. "Your mama is definitely sick. In her mind, that is. She's on drugs, now. Drugs the doctor gave her to calm her down. No drugs were in her system when the doctor tested her blood. He believes she's had a breakdown of sorts. She needs professional care."

The woman's voice softened, but her eyes remained firm. "Your mama is refusing the care she needs, and we can't keep her here. We need you need to sign this form." She held the page out to CeCe. "If either of you are at least eighteen, you can sign for her."

CeCe's eyes bore into me like she wanted me to tell her what to do. More than ever, I wanted Mama to get help; but the thought of CeCe signing those papers scared me to death. I'd seen movies where people signed papers like these and never saw their loved ones again.

CeCe must have been having the same thoughts. "We've got to read them first," she said.

"That's fine. You can bring them back when you've made a decision. I'll be at the reception station."

The nurse walked out of the room, leaving us alone with

Mama. But still, I couldn't look at her. Instead, I kept my eyes on CeCe's face. She closed her eyes for a minute, as if she might have been praying. It made me think of Daddy. I missed him something fierce. Daddy prayed before, during, and after everything. I closed my eyes and prayed too.

"Come on," CeCe said, and left the room. I followed her to the reception station, where the nurse stood talking to the clerk. CeCe walked up to her. "If I sign these papers, does it mean you can keep her here for good?"

"Heavens no," she answered. "We don't have the . . . special facilities for someone in your mama's condition. The doctor will determine where she should receive treatment. Does she have medical insurance?"

"Yes," CeCe said.

She formed a check mark with her pen. "Do you have her medical card with you?"

CeCe looked toward me. I shook my head no.

"We need her insurance information or she'll be billed," the nurse said. "In the meantime, I need those papers signed as soon as possible."

"Why do I have to sign them?" CeCe asked the nurse suspiciously.

"Your mama refused to sign anything." She gave us a

sympathetic nod. "It just states that you are responsible for payment if the insurance doesn't pay."

CeCe gasped. "I can't pay any hospital bills."

"If she has insurance, they will pay, don't worry." The nurse smiled reassuringly.

Though I was not reassured, and I know CeCe wasn't either.

"In the meantime, we will continue to ask your mama to sign the papers to admit herself." The nurse covered Mama's feet with the blanket. "If she doesn't, we'll have to bring her medical status before the judge, and he'll make the final decision."

"The judge! Why does the judge decide what becomes of my mama? She hasn't done anything wrong," I said.

"It's complicated," the nurse replied. "Do you have an older family member?"

CeCe and I both turned away, ashamed no one in our family was available to help us.

"No, ma'am, it's just us," I said, turning back around.

The nurse handed CeCe a pen. "Well, I suggest you read these papers and sign them so your mama can get the proper help."

There was a small table and chairs nearby. CeCe sat down and read the papers. She handed them to me. I glanced over them, but I didn't have the mindset to comprehend all the words floating on the pages. "Just do what you think is best," I said.

"But what Mama's insurance doesn't pay, I'll be responsible for payment!" CeCe's eyes widened. "I can't pay Mama's medical bills," CeCe said in a loud whisper.

"Don't worry. Her insurance will pay," I reassured her. "They paid for your tonsillectomy. They paid for Luke's broken ankle. And they paid for my root canal. They'll pay."

CeCe held the pen near the signature line, about to sign, but stopped and took the papers back to the nurse. "I can't sign these. I need time to think."

The nurse nodded and tilted her head in an understanding motion. "Bring them home. When you've made a decision, come back with the medical card and the forms and drop them off with the desk clerk at the entrance."

"What's gonna happen now?" CeCe asked.

"The doctor will evaluate your mama and someone will call you," she said. "There's nothing more we can do tonight." She cocked her head to the side and the kindness in her eyes made me wish she was *my* family member and I almost burst out in sobs.

The world spun around me, and I couldn't find a safe place to jump off. I glanced at CeCe, saw the dazed look on her face, and figured she felt the same. We staggered back to the car and made our way home.

CeCe went inside while I checked the mailbox. Bubbles Clayton and Miss Ruth waved hello from their front porch. *Don't they ever go anywhere?*

"Where's your mama these days?" Miss Ruth called out. "Haven't seen her around lately. She on vacation?"

If I could've shot laser beams from my eyes and knocked them both on their butts, I would've sent them flying 'cross Landon. Instead, I answered like all was fine. "No, Ma'am, she's not on vacation. I guess y'all are like two ships passin' in the night. Bye now." *You nosy old biddy.*

We hadn't eaten since lunch, and it was past 9:00. CeCe boiled up hot dogs, and we ate them smothered in ketchup on sliced bread. Afterward, I cleaned the table and CeCe laid the medical papers out. She kept tapping her nails on the table while she stared down at them. It made the moment more dramatic with each tap sounding like time was of the essence and we'd better make a decision quick.

"I can't do it," she blurted out. "I'm afraid." She stopped tapping and banged her fist on the kitchen table.

I didn't disagree. Mama needed help. I knew if it were me, I would have felt just as scared, but how could I not sign the papers if that's what needed to be done to help Mama? CeCe had done all she could. I felt bad she had to make so many decisions.

"It's okay," I said and sat down on the living room floor and alphabetized my cassette collection, which I had mixed together with the ones daddy had left behind. I listened to all of them except for the Beatles. I couldn't bear to play those tapes. I grabbed a copy of *Black and Blue* by The Rolling Stones and shoved it into my purse. I felt like listening to something that reflected my mood.

* * *

The next morning, the three of us trekked back to the hospital and parked the car. Luke had fallen asleep in the back seat.

"Should we leave him?" CeCe whispered to me.

I glanced back at Luke. "What's the sense in waking him?"

"We can't just leave him sleeping like this. What if he wakes up, he'll be scared." CeCe reached over the seat and rubbed Luke's back. "Luke. We're going inside the hospital. Do you want to come, or stay here 'til we come back?"

He grunted. "Sleep."

"Fine," CeCe said. "I'm too tired to force him. Let him be."

"He'll be all right," I said.

We locked the car doors and left Luke behind. I hadn't checked myself in the mirror all day, and I don't think CeCe had either. Strands of dark hair had fallen loose from the rubber band that tied her hair back. Now it fell past her shoulders, wavy and tangled. Pale-faced like Mama, with no make-up and her clothes wrinkled, she still could turn any guy's head.

I wanted so badly to go to school, see my friends, and wrap my arms around Matt's neck and hide my face in his soft dark hair. But every time I felt sorry for myself, I felt immediate guilt about Mama afterwards.

Once we got out of the car, we went inside and approached the front desk. This time, a different clerk sat behind it, forcing CeCe to share our story all over again. She did so calmly, but the tired and defeated expression on her face spoke volumes.

"Hold on," the clerk said. "I'll check her status."

We sat down, both crossing our right leg over our left knee. When the clerk returned, her sympathetic look told us we didn't want to hear what she had to say.

"I'm sorry, but your mama's been transferred." The desk clerk fumbled nervously with the papers in her hand.

CeCe's jaw dropped. "Transferred? But we were just here last night."

"A room became available, and the doctor saw fit your mama should have it."

CeCe jumped up from the chair. "I thought someone was

going to call us! And the night nurse told us she needed my mama's medical card—"

"We still need her card, but the doctor already petitioned the court, and the judge committed her."

"Where is she?" CeCe asked.

"Central State Hospital in Milledgeville." The nurse faced the floor afraid to meet our eyes.

Sweat poured off CeCe's forehead. Pain gripped my gut like a squirrel on an acorn. The thought of Mama held in the place once known as "Georgia's Lunatic Asylum" scared me sick. We'd both heard stories about the place as kids. I closed my eyes and prayed they were just that: made-up tales. My mind pictured something else.

CHAPTER 9

R ain splattered onto the windshield. CeCe turned on the wipers. The rubber on the passenger side wiper had torn from the metal and followed slowly behind. It made a wretched scraping sound with each stroke as it attempted to clear the rain.

Luke continued to sleep soundly.

CeCe swiped the windshield with the palm of her hand, breaking up the fog. The rain poured down harder. She sat so close to the windshield, I feared she'd go right through it if we stopped short for a possum or herd of cattle.

"Can you see?" I said.

"I can see fine, I just need to think. Stop worrying, will ya!"

"What are you worrying about?" Luke said, stretching his

arms as he woke up.

CeCe glanced at me. I could tell she didn't want to be the one to share the news. So I did.

"We have to go to another hospital. They transferred Mama."

"Is it far?"

CeCe shrugged. "I don't think it's much more than an hour away."

Luke's eyes darted back and forth, and I could see he was biting the inside of his cheek. "Is she gonna be all right?"

"Sure," CeCe answered. "She'll be fine. It might take a little time, but she'll be okay."

He put on a brave face. I could tell. I could also tell he depended on us to take care of things because we were all *he* had. Boys didn't express their feelings the way girls did, Mama always said. But I knew how Luke felt. I knew, because she was his mama as much as ours, and that would never change. You only get one mama, and I wished more than ever that I could have mine back.

I dug deep into my pocket and pulled out some Jujubes. "Here, Luke." I handed him the small box. "They probably moved Mama there so she'll get better faster. This hospital specializes in helping people like her. It's for the best. I bet she's already doing better. We might even get to take her home—"

"We need to get gas," CeCe said.

No longer consoling Luke, I switched back to my paranoid self. "There's no gas stations out here!" I said, fearing we'd break down near a chicken farm and be lost for days while Mama became a ward of the state.

"There has to be!" CeCe said, raising her voice.

The car bucked. "Are we running out of gas? We can't run out of gas here. What are we gonna do? My heartbeat quickened once more.

"Shut up, Olivia. Think positive."

The car bucked again. I began to pray. Oh, please Lord, don't let us run out of gas. "Pray, CeCe, pray!"

"I am, Olivia."

CeCe turned the high beams on, slowed down, and moved closer to the windshield as if by doing so her body's energy would magically push the car ahead.

Just as I envisioned our whole lives falling apart, we saw a gas station off to the right. CeCe pulled in and turned off the engine. She got out, pumped the gas, and handed the attendant six dollars in change.

"That's not enough money to get us there and back." I dug inside my purse and pulled out the twenty-dollar bill Jonzie had given me for my birthday. I was saving it for a new outfit for Christmas. "Here, use this."

CeCe looked surprised. "Where did you get that?"

"Don't worry about it, just take it."

CeCe accepted the bill. "Thanks."

After a few more miles on the road, she yelled, "I see a sign. Five more miles and we'll be there."

She turned off the highway and drove what seemed more like fifty miles before we saw civilization again.

We drove past an old Civil War building on a hill overlooking several acres of pecan trees. Deteriorated red brick structures with rusted bars covering broken windowpanes smothered with Kudzu surrounded the place. The iron gates were open, but not welcoming. Once we passed the gate, we drove by unmarked graves, lined in rows on the grassy grounds. I didn't even want to think why the graves might be there.

A vision of Mama, dirty-faced and dressed in a white hospital gown popped into my head. Each sickening thought dug up every ugly memory I'd ever had. I *hated* to imagine Mama in this place. I *hated* that no one in our family came to help us. I couldn't understand how God could take Daddy away and leave our mama without her mind.

And I hated not knowing what would come next.

I peered down as I felt my tears fall onto the skin of my knee. Without realizing it, I'd picked at the small hole in my jeans. Now, it was the size of an apple. *Better than picking more eyelashes,* I thought.

* * *

The second we entered the admissions area, my eyes connected with an old woman. With matted hair and dark circles under her eyes, she reminded me of a character straight from an old horror film. Any moment I feared she would turn into a monster and grab me by the throat.

She turned away quickly and stared out the window as if she were contemplating smashing her frail body through it, or maybe mine. I sneezed, and she whirled back around. By then I had fixed my eyes on the television hanging in the corner.

"Have you seen my daughter?" she said.

Taken aback by the agony revealed in her pale blue eyes, I glanced at her and said, "No Ma'am, I'm sorry."

She sunk her chin down into her neck and continued down the hallway. A man dressed in a white buttoned-up jacket wearing a hospital nametag approached us and took her gently by the arm. "Let's go back to recreation, Minta." She joined the group of patients he was leading, and they faded into the distance as they shuffled away.

"Can I help you?"

I swiveled around and faced a glass window where the heavyset black woman behind it asked the question.

CeCe pulled Mama's medical card out of her purse and presented it. "We're here about our mother. She was transferred from Henry Medical Center last night."

"What's her name?"

"Cassandra Travis." CeCe swallowed and gazed directly into the woman's eyes.

"You'll have to take a seat. I'll call her caseworker. He'll be down shortly."

CeCe nodded. "Thank you."

Like ducks, Luke and I followed her to the small waiting area and sat in the plastic chairs.

Time crept as we waited.

"I'm hungry," Luke said.

I turned to him and noticed that his face seemed thinner than usual. Tall and lanky, he needed a constant flow of food to keep his body ticking. Even though I couldn't muster up an appetite, it was a good thing that Luke could.

CeCe reached inside her pocket and put some change down on the table. I guess she saved some extra since I had given her the twenty. "Here, go get something from the vending machine."

She pointed to the far corner of the room.

Luke gathered the change and took off, passing a bald man wearing a white shirt and tie and carrying a clipboard. The man spoke to the desk clerk and then approached us.

He extended his arm. "Hello, my name is Walter Shimmering. I'm the caseworker for your mother."

"Caseworker? What's a caseworker?" I asked him. "Where's my mama's doctor? We want to talk to her doctor."

He relaxed from his rigid stance. I stared at the small leaf-shaped wine stain on top of his bald head. "I'm sorry, I forgot you're new to this. You *will* see her doctor. I'm the person who oversees the patient's paperwork and goes between Dr. Foster and the patient's family—"

CeCe jumped up. "What can you tell us?"

"Come to my office and we'll talk." As he said that, he pointed toward the corridor.

CeCe and I followed and waved Luke on as we passed the vending machine.

Mr. Shimmering led us into an office with a medium-sized desk that was scattered with papers. CeCe sat directly across from him. Luke and I sat down in the chairs on each side of her. A bowl filled with candy sat on the corner of his desk. Luke quickly snatched a handful and stuffed his pocket.

"First, I need some information on your mother," Mr. Shimmering said. "Does she have any allergies?"

"No," CeCe replied.

"Is she on any medication at this time?"

"No."

"Has she ever been hospitalized before?"

CeCe straightened in her seat. "Only when she gave birth to us, as far as I know."

Mr. Shimmering laid his pen down on the desk, removed his glasses, and rubbed the bridge of his nose. "Your mother is in a state of psychosis. She's heavily medicated with a medication called Haldol. She's sleeping comfortably now. But when she's awake, she becomes combative." He glanced away, then back to us, and said, "We had to restrain her."

"Restrain her?" CeCe yelped, clenching her hands together. "But my mama wouldn't hurt a fly!"

"What's *restrain* mean?" Luke whispered behind CeCe's back.

"Tell you later," I said to him.

"You have to remember, she's not in her regular state of mind," Mr. Shimmering continued. "She's not acting like 'your mama' right now."

"So what *exactly* is wrong with her?" I said as soon as he

stopped for a breath.

A long pause later, he said, "At this point in time, the doctor has diagnosed her with schizophrenia. But he's still doing tests."

I knew it, I thought, remembering the talk show. Now, I didn't want to believe it.

The phone rang, and Mr. Shimmering held up his finger. "One minute."

I stared at CeCe. Her eyes looked hard at work trying not to cry. I thought I'd be glad when a doctor confirmed my beliefs. But I decided not to believe him, at least for a while. *It could be something else*, I thought. *Maybe a brain aneurism, even.*

We all sat staring at Mr. Shimmering, urging him with our eyes to hang up the phone. Finally, he did.

"Where was I? Oh, yes, the doctor has diagnosed your mother with paranoid schizophrenia."

Paranoid. He didn't say that the first time, only schizophrenia.

"I know, you said that already," CeCe reminded him. "What are you going to do to fix it?"

Mr. Shimmering's face turned pale. "I'm sorry, but this is not like a broken arm. It can't be fixed." He scratched his red leaf. "It can be controlled—with the right medication, of course."

"What is the right medication?" CeCe asked.

"It's not that simple," he said. "Each person responds differently to medication. Where one works for one patient, it might not for another. We need to keep her here awhile so we can monitor her."

CeCe turned around and looked toward Luke and me. What could we say? What could we do? We were at the mercy of the hospital and this mannequin of a man as our information advisor. CeCe, Luke, and I couldn't take care of Mama anymore; we had to leave her so the doctors could. And although I worried about Mama, thoughts of my own future still ran through my head; and I hated myself for it.

CHAPTER 10

At that moment, I realized more decisions and chores lay ahead of us. We had to tell Mama's manager at the nursing home she was sick. We had to make sure all the bills were paid or we'd lose the stinking trailer. We had to get some food for Luke before he ended up in the hospital too.

"Can we see her?" CeCe asked.

Mr. Shimmering turned a page in his day planner and said, "Visiting hours begin at 2:00." He glanced at his watch. "It's only 1:00. Why don't you go to the cafeteria and grab some lunch."

Luke perked up. I couldn't remember when I'd last eaten. I doubted CeCe could either, or cared.

"What did you say her doctor's name was?" CeCe asked Mr. Shimmering.

"Dr. Foster. You'll meet him when he checks in on your mother." He backed his chair away from his desk and stood, extended his arm again to CeCe and handed her his business card. "If you have any questions, call me at this number."

CeCe nodded and the three of us left the office. We roamed the hallways following signs for the cafeteria. Every so often we would see a group of people following a nurse. Sometimes we'd see someone wandering alone.

Luke scanned the wide selection of food in the cafeteria. I caught him filling his pockets with cookies and candy, but I didn't say anything. CeCe and I took a container of yogurt and a Coke. She reached inside her pocket and came out with a few coins. Then she looked at me. I held my palms up and shrugged. CeCe put the Coke back and used the last bit of change for the yogurt and handed it to me. We sat down at a table and waited quietly until 2:00.

Finally, we walked back to the front desk. A woman told us Mama's room number. We wandered down the long hallway, peeking inside rooms with opened doors. We saw old people, black people, young people, and people like Mama. Though they were all different, they all had the same vacant look in their eyes.

I stopped at the doorway and glanced inside Mama's room. She was lying in the bed with her back facing the door. The other side of the room held an empty bed. On her bedside table a tray of food lay, untouched.

CeCe shoved me inside and Luke followed.

"Hi, Mama," CeCe said softly. "How ya feelin'?"

She rolled over and propped herself up. Still dirty, but not as dirty as before. No restraints held her down like Mr. Shimmering had told us there would be. She brushed her knotted hair behind her ears. As she did, I noticed the pink fingernail manicure CeCe had given her last week was chipped and jagged. My heart ached seeing her this way. It reminded me of the day she dug the Thanksgiving turkey out of the garden.

"How did I get here?" she asked hard and fast.

"You got lost, Mama," CeCe said. We tried to find you, but the police found you first."

"The police found you and brought you to Henry Hospital," I added. "Then they took you here without telling us."

She hit the mattress with her fists. "Why! Why . . . why, here?" she yelled in a high-pitched voice. "I've gotta get outta here." She began squirming. "Olivia, give me your compact." The tone of her voice deepened. "Do you know where I am? Do you!"

CeCe began to cry. "I know, Mama, I know. I never wanted you to come here. I wanted you to come home. But when I brought your medical card back to the hospital, they'd already taken you."

"Get me a brush, Olivia. I need to fix my hair, and you need to take me home."

CeCe handed her the brush from her purse, but then closed her eyes, as if she was afraid to meet Mama's harsh stare. "We can't."

"What do you mean you can't? I said take me home. Now, dammit!"

Out of nowhere, the brush, her hand clasped around it, whipped across CeCe's face. She placed her hand over her cheek and ran out of the room sobbing. My heart sunk. Mama had never hit any of us before. *Combative . . . restrain . . .* I understood now, and knew it was time for me to take my place on the proverbial seesaw. For CeCe's sake.

"Luke, go tend to CeCe," I ordered.

He was glad to go. He nearly ran out of the room.

"You only have to stay here for a little while, Mama," I said. "Just until the doctor finds the right medicine for you. To help you remember things again."

Mama slouched down in the bed and lifted the blankets to her neck. "You're all ganging up on me. What did I do to deserve this? You want to hurt me. Why do you want to hurt me?" She asked like a child - wide-eyed and confused.

"Nobody wants to hurt you, Mama. We want to help you," I told her.

Footsteps came up behind me and I turned to see a doctor enter the room.

"How are we doing, Cassandra?" he said to Mama. "I'm Dr. Foster. I'm here to help you."

She rolled over and faced the wall. The doctor pulled a seat up to her bed and faced her. Luke walked back into the room with CeCe shuffling hesitantly behind him. A red streak from the brush slap ran down her left cheek.

"These must be your children," he said, and smiled.

Mama continued to face the wall. "Yes. They've come to take me home."

Dr. Foster wrote on his notepad. "Well, that's nice you have a loving family. And they'll be able to take you home real soon. We just need to find the right medication for you first."

Mama sat up and pushed the tray of food away from the bed. The silver plate cover fell to the floor. I flinched.

"I don't need medicine," she shouted. "I need to go home."

The doctor reached over to console her. She jerked forward and bit his hand. He yanked it away. Red-faced, he yelled, "Nurse!"

"I'll hurt you before I let you hurt me!" Mama said. "CeCe, Livia . . . "

The nurse rushed into the room with an orderly at her side. The orderly pushed Mama's shoulders down and restrained her while the nurse gave her a shot. By this time, each of us could hear each other stifling our cries.

Mama's eyes rolled back in her head, and within a minute she was asleep. Dr. Foster told us to follow him to his office while he wrapped his hand with a gauze bandage the nurse gave him.

We sat down again and listened to a bunch of long words that ran into one another. Instead of listening and trying to understand the doctor, I started spelling the words in my mind. After he finished, he stared at us and there was an awkward silence. I don't know what CeCe was thinking, but I wished the doctor from the TV show was there. He had made things much easier to understand.

I figured he must have realized we were lost in his medical montage and began speaking again, slower and more direct this time. "Mental illness is a very complex disease. I'm not certain of my diagnosis. It's difficult to determine whether your mother is manic-depressive, schizoaffective, or a paranoid schizophrenic. She's not cooperating. I'll need your help to learn about the time and frequency of her episodes."

CeCe and I stared at one another. Although I'd heard these terms before, I never expected the doctor to ask us to help him figure out how to help Mama. He was the doctor. Why was he asking us?

CeCe recovered faster than I did. She stood up and pointed her finger at him.

"Sir, could you please explain to us in *our* language what you're doing to help our mother?"

"I'm sorry," he said. "The bottom line is our first priority is to bring your mother out of the psychotic state she's in."

"What exactly is *psychotic*?" CeCe asked.

Although I knew the answer after watching the TV show, I stayed quiet. CeCe needed to hear it from the doctor. I guess I did, too. Then there would be no way of denying it.

"It's when a patient loses touch with reality. Your mother doesn't process things the way you and I do. She may seem as if she does from time to time, but it'll be short-lived. And it will be only a matter of time before she does something that may cause herself or someone else harm."

CeCe took a deep breath and regained her composure. "I'm sorry for losing my temper. It's just . . . this is new for us, and we're all a bit scared. We just want to know when our mother will be well again."

"It will take some time. Most patients stay up to thirty days. When we find a medication that works for your mother, we'll continue with it until we believe she's fit to go home. We also combine medication with psychotherapy." He smiled. "Another big word. Psychotherapy is working with her individually and in groups so she can express her feelings to help us understand what's going on in her mind."

I knew what psychotherapy was, but I didn't want Dr. Foster to think I had an attitude, so I acted as if everything he said was new to me. He looked from CeCe to Luke, then to me, then back to CeCe. "The best thing you can all do is go home and let us do our job. We'll let you know of your Mama's progress. You can see her during visiting hours."

The doctor showed compassion in his voice, but I could tell he made that same speech hundreds of times.

He stood and extended his hand. CeCe shook it like it was contaminated, and we left. We traveled the long ride home quietly, but my mind was filled with noise. Like a hundred people talking at once with one of those people yelling above them all. And it was me. *CeCe, you can't go away. Ever. Mama will always be sick and I can't take care of her without you.*

CHAPTER 11

My two front teeth fell out. I ripped at the carpet fiercely, trying to find them. Then I was sitting at my desk, Monica Bradshaw throwing Jujubes at me, laughing and yelling, "Stick these in your mouth." She sat behind Matt, running her fingers through his curly hair as pieces of candy fell to the ground. . . .

I woke up drenched with sweat, still seeing Matt's face. It was noon. Luke and CeCe were already up. We had missed two days of school and I still hadn't told anyone about Mama, though CeCe told Mama's boss, who was kind and understanding.

I sat down at the kitchen table. CeCe was making grits on the stove. She put the pot aside and said, "Olivia, I think I should call your guidance counselor at school."

My eyes widened. "Absolutely not! I don't need to talk to her about this. This is a private family matter." My guidance counselor liked me. She told me I had a future . . . potential. I didn't want her to know about Mama. It might change the way she thought about me.

CeCe turned to Luke. "How 'bout you? Do you want me to speak to your guidance counselor?"

He shrugged. "What for?"

"Because—even though Mama's in the hospital, we all have to go back to school. I know it'll be hard to concentrate. If your counselor knows about our . . . family matters, she'll make sure your teachers understand if you're not quite yourself."

"Go ahead, I don't care one way or the other," he said, and disappeared into his bedroom.

I knew CeCe was just trying to help, but my emotions shifted from moment to moment just like they did after Daddy died. In some ways, I felt like Mama was dying too. Random thoughts from my memory stirred throughout my mind. Thoughts about Mama when Daddy had been alive. I remembered an instance when we'd gotten to church once and Daddy made us all leave the moment we took off our coats and sat down. Mama had been wearing her nightgown instead of her dress.

After that, a flash went through my mind of Daddy squeezing toothpaste onto Mama's toothbrush. Her teeth were blue and she was holding a tube of icing from Luke's first birthday cake. It all seemed like a dream now, but I knew it had happened.

Then I reminisced about the time Mama first told us we had to sell the house and move into the trailer. I gave her an awful time about it. I refused to let anyone know about our move for as long as possible. The thought of someone calling me "trailer trash" crushed my ego. I despised the term before we moved and after we had, I feared it.

I shouldn't have given her a hard time. I should have realized she was fragile, and I knew then, I should have shared my feelings with someone back when Daddy died. Maybe it might have helped fill the void in my heart now. But it was too late. Instead, I found other ways to fill it. I sought out Matt. He'd called over the weekend and left a message on the answering machine to see how I was doing. Bessa and Jonzie left messages too, but I didn't feel like talking to them just yet.

I snuck Mama's car keys out of her purse. Although I knew how to drive, I didn't have a license. Matt only lived fifteen minutes away. I figured it wouldn't be a big deal. It was well after suppertime and I didn't think I'd be intruding.

When I reached his neighborhood, I couldn't help but covet the beautiful homes, wishing I lived in one of them instead of our puny trailer. Monica Bradshaw lived down the road from him, in a house about the same size. I couldn't bear the thought of her seeing me get out of Mama's car. Her cherry bomb tank, an old Oldsmobile, stuck out like a cow on a pig farm. So I parked a block away.

Since I appeared more desirable than the last time he had seen me, I hoped Matt would be happily surprised. No cars sat parked in the driveway. I figured his parents were gone, and maybe we'd have an opportunity to finish where we had left off the night of the concert.

My nerves jumped like grasshoppers inside the pit of my stomach, but it would be worth it, I told myself. I locked Bessa's advice out of my head, rang the doorbell, and waited. No one answered. I pressed it again and put my ear to the door. Music played, and I heard footsteps.

Finally, the door opened and a tall voluptuous girl around CeCe's age stood there. Although Matt and I had been dating a couple of months, I didn't really know him as well as I thought I had. I didn't even know if he had brothers and sisters. I figured the girl at the door must be his sister. I gave her a nervous smile. "Hi, I'm Olivia, Matt isn't expecting me, but I was in the neighborhood and I thought I'd stop by. Is he home?"

A pair of dark chocolate eyes coated in lavender shadow

and liquid liner examined me thoroughly. She called up the stairs in a raspy voice, "Matt, you have a visitor."

He came to the front door, wearing blue jeans and no shirt. Not much different than the last time I'd seen him.

"Olivia, what's up? Watcha doin' here?" He didn't seem happy or unhappy to see me. But, he didn't seem like the Matt I was with on Saturday night. And I had an inkling that Miss Liner Lids wasn't his sister after she stepped behind him and wrapped her arms around his waist. "Hurry up, Matt," she said. "I wanna get started."

I swallowed hard. "I . . . I just wanted to say sorry for the other night. I'll see ya." I turned to leave.

"Wait!" He placed his hand on my shoulder. An angry warm feeling ran through my body. I turned back around to see him running his fingers through the top of his dark curls. "Why didn't you call?"

"I wanted to surprise you," I said, holding back tears.

"Come on, Matt. I'm waiting," the smoky voice called, now from upstairs.

"I gotta go," I said, and turned around.

"No, wait!"

I marched down the steps, not turning back, and listened for the door to close.

I sprinted around the corner toward the car, slid behind the wheel, stuck the key in the ignition, and turned the radio to blasting levels. I stepped down on the gas. The Rolling Stones song *Paint it Black* played and the music fueled my anger. I sang along. . . . *Black as night, black as coal, I wanna see the sun blotted out from the sky, I wanna see it painted, painted, painted black . . .*

My mind kept replaying the last moments: Matt with no shirt, the girl's hands wrapped around his waist. Her voice calling him from upstairs. Long legs, dark eyes, fuchsia lips.

Red lights.

In my rearview mirror, I saw them and snapped out of my pity party. I peered down at the speedometer and it read eighty miles an hour. I slowed down and pulled to the side of the road. By the time the police officer appeared, my emotional levee broke and tears rushed down my face. I cried. I cried until the salt from my tears gagged me.

The officer tapped my window with his stick. I rolled it down and glared up at him with my tearstained face. He reminded me of the police officer who came to our door the night Daddy died, the one who stared at his shoes while the older one told us the news. And this one was going to take me to jail because I was speeding, and I didn't even have a license. It couldn't get any worse than this. Did God hate me?

"Are you okay, young lady?" he asked.

"No! No! No!" I cried. "I just left my mother at Central State Hospital, and I don't know what I'm gonna do."

He handed me his handkerchief. I gazed up at him and sniffled. "Thank you, Sir."

Instead of scolding me and giving me a ticket, he said, "Do yourself a favor. Slow down, and get on home." He tipped his hat in the same way the officer did when Mama whispered in his ear the day the stranger slipped out our back door.

"Thank you, Lord," I whispered after he stepped away, feeling guilty I'd had such blasphemous thoughts.

My tears had not fallen in vain. Had the police officer asked to see my license I don't know what would've happened. Except that one more stressful incident would have sent me over to Central State with Mama.

I took the officer's advice and drove home slowly. When I reached the trailer, I staggered to my side of the bed and collapsed.

The next morning, I hit the snooze button one too many times and overslept. I hadn't heard CeCe get up, which was surprising since it was impossible not to hear or feel every move each other made having shared a bed for four long years.

After I showered, I cleared the mirror and stared at my swollen eyes. In no mood for the third degree I knew I'd get from Jonzie and Bessa, I plotted an excuse as I pulled on my jeans, which seemed to have grown a size. I tossed them aside. And for the first time, I was able to slide on a pair of CeCe's size three jeans. Strange how something so inane boosted my mood. Maybe I'd borrow CeCe's black pants too, I thought. We finished breakfast, and each of us parted ways and went about our routines, knowing in the back of our minds our mama lay trapped in a mental institution.

Jonzie spotted me in homeroom and headed to me like a bee to a daffodil. "Where've you been? I called a bunch of times and nobody answered."

"My mama accidentally turned off the ringer," I lied.

Jonzie scrunched her eyebrows. "You could've called me!"

"Sorry."

"And what's wrong with your eyes?"

"I got pinkeye," I said, and faced the floor.

Jonzie put her hand on her hip. "In both eyes? Who do you think you're talking to? What happened with Matt?"

"It's a long story."

"Well, tell me the short version. Did you do it or not?"

The bell rang, and I collected my books and started for the

door. I didn't move fast enough. She followed me into the hallway.

"You did. Didn't you?" She grinned.

I refused to discuss anything about my personal life in the school hallway, and only said, "No."

"What do you mean, 'No'? *No* you didn't do it? Or *no*, it wasn't good? I'm not going to class until you tell me the whole story."

I drew in a breath and let it out. "Well, unless you want to come with me to English, you're not getting it until later." I knew English was the last place Jonzie would follow me, so I walked faster.

She placed her hand on her right hip. "Fine, I'll meet you later."

"Fine," I mimicked. As great a friend as Jonzie was, she was equally draining at times.

School had always come easy to me, and most teachers liked me, probably because of my fame as a star student and winning every spelling bee from grammar school through ninth grade. There'd been a time when my goal in life had been to obtain a scholarship. To where, I wasn't sure. And for what? After learning about Mama's condition, maybe I'd think about becoming a psychiatrist.

But deep inside I dreamed of becoming a TV talk-show host, or maybe a journalist like Diane Sawyer. I'd dig up information about corruption, famous stars gone bad, and interview dignitaries. People would fawn all over me before my show - applying my makeup, fixing my hair, feeding me information through an earpiece about my latest guest while my audience hung on my every word.

I would never share my dream with CeCe or Mama. CeCe was the star of the family. Neither of them would take me seriously. I hadn't even participated in any spelling bees since ninth grade. And no one except my guidance counselor had ever asked about my plans for my future. It seemed my place in our family was to remain in the middle . . . the middle of eternal chaos.

Class flew by and the bell rang, and my stomach lurched again. It was time for lunch and an interrogation from Bessa and Jonzie. But I figured it would be easier to talk about Matt than Mama, so I let it all out.

* * *

"Just because he was with that girl doesn't mean he doesn't still like you," Jonzie said. "You got him all worked up and he needed to find an experienced skier." She giggled and put her hand on my arm. "It's okay. You're not the first girl who's gotten drunk and puked at the feet of a gorgeous hunk of a guy."

I pulled my arm back. "Stifle it, Jonzie."

"Oh, I'm just teasing. He's a jerk, but there's no doubt he's got it for you. Lust swims in his eyes when he plants them on your perfect . . . little . . . behind . . ."

"Praise the Lord!" Bessa interrupted. "I prayed that God would intercede and keep you from giving away the precious sanctity of your virginity." She smiled at me and smirked at Jonzie. "You said it, Jonzie. Lust . . . not love."

Even if what Jonzie said was true, how could I be with Matt now? In spite of my worries about everything else, anger and jealousy enveloped me. Regardless of Matt's hunky status, I no longer intended on *skiing* with him. Maybe Bessa was right, and God stopped me before I had a chance to jump into the water.

"Look! There he is." Jonzie nodded in his direction.

I bent down and pretended to pick up my pencil so he wouldn't see me.

"He's looking for you," Jonzie whispered. "Those dark urban eyes are seeking you out. Get up, girl."

"Let him keep seeking," I said, and kept my head down. A few seconds later, I asked, "Is he gone yet?"

Before Jonzie could answer, I shot up from beneath the

table and banged my forehead. Hot breath swished down the back of my neck. I turned around, and the scorching breath became warm lips on my bruised forehead while firm hands pulled me to a standing position. Bessa and Jonzie sat in silent shock. Face-to-face with Matt, I stood dumfounded. He boasted a wide grin as if he'd never been in his house with another girl while I stood at his front door like an idiot.

"What's up?" he asked through his grin.

I stepped back and turned away from his magnetic eyes. "Nothing."

"Why'd you run off the other night?"

I placed my hands on my hips. "How stupid do you think I am?"

I sat back down at the table and reached over to Bessa. "Pass me the ketchup, please."

Matt frowned. "Why would I think you're stupid?"

I dipped my fry in the ketchup and stirred it around my plate.

"I don't think she wants to talk to you," Bessa said.

"Do you want to talk to me?" he asked me.

I growled at him with my eyes.

"Told you," Bessa said, gloating.

"I want you to come to a party Saturday night. My band is

112

playing." He bent down to my level, tilted his head, and shot me his famous, crooked smile. I kept my eyes on the fries. He remained there for a few seconds, then straightened his posture. "Call me."

He strutted away and Jonzie kicked me underneath the table. "How can you have so much will power? He is so fine."

"Enough already!" I don't care how fine he is, he cheated on me the first chance he got."

Jonzie lowered her eyelids and shrunk down in her seat.

All I had to do was think about Mama lying in that hospital bed and even Matt couldn't hurt me anymore. When Mama invaded my mind, I felt cold and numb. I could tune out just about everything, even in a crowded room with my best friends.

When I snapped out of my thoughts, I looked up, and Jonzie raised her right eyebrow and glared at me. "There's more to this story than you're telling us, and I aim to find out."

The lunch bell rang, saving me.

CHAPTER 12

After school, I placed my books on the kitchen table, grabbed a few chocolate chip cookies, and plopped down on the couch like usual. I stared at the telephone for a few minutes, willing Matt to call, even though he told me to call *him*. If he did call, I'd hang up on him anyway.

After about half an hour into *General Hospital*, I wondered why Luke wasn't home yet. I checked his room. His schoolbooks lay on the bed. Either he skipped out early or he didn't go to school at all.

I threw on my coat and headed down the street toward the woods behind the trailer park. Something told me I'd find him there. I shuffled through the leaves and snapped back branches. Sure enough, I smelled cigarettes and could hear young male voices, laughing and joking. Four of them sat in a row on the trunk of a fallen tree, passing chips, soda, and cigarettes back and forth. The scene appeared harmless at first, until a boy stood up and smashed a rock to the ground. Everyone cheered.

Someone shouted. "Harder! Break the sucker open!"

A lanky boy with scraggly cinnamon colored hair smashed a rock against . . .

A parking meter? They stole a parking meter?

Strange as that sounded in my head, that was the only way a parking meter could've possibly ended up in the middle of the woods.

When the rock didn't break it open, the boy stormed away, flipping his middle finger up in frustration. "Go ahead, Luke, you try," he said.

Scowling, Luke picked up a brick from the ground and bashed the parking meter. Cheers and roars applauded him. The glass of the meter cracked, but the part that held the money remained intact.

An older boy, maybe the leader of the group, said, "Aww, close, Luke, but no cigar."

I marched up to Luke and grabbed him by the collar. "We have to go."

All eyes turned toward me.

"You're not gonna tell, are ya?" the older boy pleaded.

I studied his face for a moment and felt his desperation. I couldn't tell if he was fearful of me telling, or determined to open the meter and get the money.

"I'm not gonna tell, but y'all are gonna get in a lot of trouble if you get caught."

"You ain't gonna tell. So we ain't gonna get caught," the older boy said, and the others laughed.

"See ya, Luke." Each boy waved, and another took his turn at cracking the meter.

As we shuffled through the leaves, I whispered in Luke's ear, "What the heck were you thinking!"

He stared toward the ground while he played foot hockey with acorns. "I didn't steal it. They already had it when I got there."

"Didn't you ever hear of an accessory to a crime?"

He looked up at me. "A what?"

I shook my head. "Being with those boys and trying to break that meter open makes you just as guilty as the one who stole it."

Luke seemed deaf to my words. I couldn't believe it. He cared so much about the money he didn't even care what could've happened to him if he got caught!

But then again, CeCe and I hadn't been the best examples.

Once we got home, Luke walked to the refrigerator, grabbed a Coke, sat at the table and emptied his pockets. He spread out a pile of candy.

"Where'd you get all that?" I asked.

"It must have fallen into my pockets at Piggly Wiggly." He chuckled and shrugged.

He almost seemed proud of what he'd done. Luke was slowly changing. Stealing now became the norm for him instead of something he did because CeCe asked him to out of necessity, although that wasn't right either. It was obvious his behavior needed to be dealt with, but I didn't know what to do. I didn't think CeCe could handle another thing on her plate. And I was right. When she walked in a minute later, dark circles and pale skin added years to her eighteen-year-old face, and despite everything, I blurted out, "Luke's been stealing." Then I told her what I found him doing in the woods.

She laid her coat on the couch and bore into Luke's face with angry eyes. "What the heck's wrong with you, boy? You can't be doing stuff like this. It's wrong!" She banged her fist on the table.

He gave her a narrow stare. "You're the one who taught me to steal. What do you care?"

"Don't get ugly with me, Luke." By then confusion and

guilt crossed her face. She breathed for a moment, and then lightened her tone. "Luke, I never wanted you to steal Mama's car. I only did it because I didn't know what else to do at the time. I don't claim to know everything or to always have the right answers, but I do know those boys you're hanging with are trouble. And stealing things like parking meters will send you to jail. Think about your future. Think about Mama—"

"Mama's stinkin' crazy," he shot back. "Grandma and Grandpa don't give a crap. And Daddy's dead. I don't care what happens to me!" He gathered the candy from the table, stuffed it back into his pockets, and left the house. The door slammed shut behind him.

Just like always, I turned to CeCe. "What are we gonna do?"

With the movements of an old woman, she lowered herself into the chair Luke just vacated and folded her hands in front of her. "It's true. It *is* my fault. I could've found another way for us to get money, or get Mama's car. Instead, I'm turning my little brother into a criminal. I hate myself." She folded her arms, rested them on the table and buried her face beneath them and started to cry.

CeCe had always been the one to uplift Luke and me. Lately our roles seemed to be shifting. I sat next to her and placed my hand on her shoulder. "It's not your fault. If you knew a better way, you would have found it. It's not like we planned any of those things, or had time to figure them out. You just did the best you could."

She lifted her head. Her eyes were closed, but I could see she'd stopped crying. I knew she was worn down. And I couldn't imagine how hard it was for her to carry the burdens she did. We needed someone else to help us before our family completely fell apart.

I racked my brain trying to think of whom else we could go to. I don't know how long I sat there, but when I glanced at CeCe again, she'd fallen asleep with her head on the kitchen table and I had a glob of mascara and four eyelashes between my thumb and forefinger.

CHAPTER 13

The telephone rang and startled CeCe awake. I tried to grab the phone before it woke her, but she jumped up and knocked into me as she grabbed the receiver.

"No, Cassandra isn't here right now. Can I take a message? Okay, bye." She turned to me. "Who the heck is Westin Barnes?"

My eyes widened. "I can't believe it! It's that man who drove Mama home when she lost her car. The guy who was in her bedroom!"

"He sounded kind of nice."

I smirked. "Nice? Give me a break."

"No, I mean it," she said. "There was . . . something in his voice."

I shrugged. "Well, it doesn't matter anyway, Mama's not

here."

CeCe went to the couch and finished her nap. I thought about Matt again. Before, thoughts of him could take my mind off Mama. Now there was no place my mind could go for rest. I couldn't forgive Matt and go to that party. I'd look pathetic and desperate. I needed a new distraction. It was time I set my sights on someone else.

The phone rang again - this time it was Jonzie.

"Maybe you can fool Bessa, but you can't fool me," she said.

"What are you talking about?"

"I saw your eyes today. I saw the same sadness I felt after Michael died. You had better tell me what's going on with you."

"Meet me at the park by the lake," I said, and hung up. I couldn't hold it all inside anymore. I *had* to talk to somebody, and since Jonzie had gone through tough times before, maybe she would understand without judging.

The phone didn't wake CeCe this time, so I left her a note. On my bike, it was a quick mile and a half to the park. Jonzie was sitting on a bench smoking a cigarette.

"When the heck did you take up that nasty habit?" I asked.

She held the pack out and offered me one.

"No thanks," I said, although I had to admit the thought of

trying one did entice me.

"It's not a habit yet," she said, the cigarette hanging from her mouth as she shoved the pack into her pocket. "I've only done it a few times. My mama took it up after Michael died. I felt like doing everything bad after that. Maybe she did too. So I thought you might want to join me." She took a drag and made a couple of smoke rings that followed each other toward the lake and disappeared.

I shook my head. "No thanks. Luke's doing enough bad things for the both of us."

"Luke? What's going on with him?"

I sat down next to her on the picnic table and put my feet up on the bench, my elbows on my knees. I shoved my fists under my cheeks and pushed them into my eyes to hold up my head. "My mama's gone crazy," I blurted out.

Jonzie took another drag from her cigarette then flicked it into the lake. "I knew that the day I met her," she said with a giggle.

Tears filled my eyes. "No. Not just mama-crazy. I mean *really* crazy. She's in the hospital."

Jonzie moved closer to me on the bench. "I'm sorry, Honey. I didn't mean any harm. Where is she?"

"She's in Central State," I said, and started bawling.

Jonzie slid her arm around me. "Oh, crap. How'd she end up there?"

"I guess it's like you said," I said between sobs and sniffles. "She's always been kind of different, but not the kind of crazy she is now. She buried our turkey on Thanksgiving. In the front yard . . . to save our souls!"

Jonzie's eyes bulged. "Whoa, that is definitely one I have not heard before. I guess that is pretty crazy!"

Leave it to Jonzie to say it like it is.

"She never really got over Daddy's death," I said. "She doesn't cry all the time like she used to, and she goes to work and all, but sometimes it's like a page is missing from her brain. And when the anniversary of his death comes around, she gets worse. She disappeared one night. The police found her, but she ended up in Central State before CeCe and I could get to her. The doctor says she has mental illness. You know what people will say about that. . . . I can't tell anyone. And you can't either!"

Jonzie got up off the bench. She paced the ground with her head down. I thought she was about to give me another lecture, like the skiing one.

"When Michael died, my mama went to Central State too. I didn't tell anyone. My daddy brought her there. She wouldn't talk, cook, clean, or do anything. She just lay around like she was dead but still breathing. I didn't even care 'cause I felt the same way." She stopped pacing and took a deep breath. "But . . . instead, I hurt myself on the outside so the inside wouldn't feel so bad."

Jonzie pushed up the right leg of her jeans and exposed the rest of her calf. Scars like ladder rungs ran from the top of the flame on her tattoo to just above her knee. I'd never noticed them before, probably because I was always gaping at her tattoo, thinking about getting one myself, or maybe because Jonzie never exposed her legs completely. She wore straight legs all the time and cuffed the bottoms so you could only see her tattoo. In gym she wore knee socks.

"Michael and I always talked about our plans. You know, we were gonna rent a camper and drive across the country after we finished high school and go to San Francisco. First we were gonna go to Alabama, then Mississippi, then stop in Arkansas and visit some friends and family. We were gonna go to Colorado and try snow skiing, then Vegas and pull the one arm bandits, and finally San Francisco and ride the cable cars. And for our ultimate goal, we planned to roller skate down Lombard Street."

Each time Jonzie mentioned one of these places, she pointed at another deep-lined scar. When she finished, she let go of her pant leg and it slid back down to her ankle.

"Whenever I felt bad, I'd think about each place that Michael and I were planning to go and I'd slash the side of my leg like I was crossing the date off a calendar. Sometimes I still do. I just ran out of states."

I pictured her in the act of doing this. Jonzie had always been rough. But to take a razor blade and deliberately slash your own leg really freaked me out.

Jonzie lit another cigarette and continued. "We visited my mama at the hospital for about a month. A doctor we met talked to us about our feelings about Michael. About trying to move on with our lives. Eventually, my mama came home. She started taking back to her old ways, but she's still not the same. I'm not either."

I sighed. "I'm sorry. I didn't know, Jonzie. How horrible it must have been for you. I felt like that when my daddy died. But we didn't have anyone to talk to or help us. We had to stop grieving so we could take care of Mama. Now she's in that stinking hospital, Luke's acting up, and CeCe is worn out."

"I know that hospital seems creepy and all, but they helped my mama, and they'll help yours." She walked over and hugged me.

"Thanks," I said. "But don't tell anyone. I hate talking

about it. All we do at home is talk about it, and although I love Bessa to bits, she'll send me to her granny or pastor." I picked up a flat stone and skipped it across the lake. "They'll just tell me to bring it to God. Well, I already have. I talk to God more than I have in a long time."

"Don't worry, I won't tell." She reached inside her pocket. "Sure you don't want a cigarette?"

I shook my head and mustered up the best grin I could. "No thanks."

Jonzie shoved the pack back into her pocket and hopped on her bike. "If you change your mind, let me know. I've got a whole carton." She shot me a devilish grin. "I'd better get home before my mama starts freakin' out." She waved and pedaled away.

"See ya," I said, and took off in the other direction. I prayed on the way. I prayed the Lord would help CeCe and me find a way to make Luke behave. I prayed God would fix Mama, and I prayed He'd make Jonzie stop hurting herself.

* * *

Jonzie kept my secret like she promised and I kept hers. Two weeks had passed since Mama was committed to the hospital. Luke and I visited a few times, but each time we were disappointed. She wasn't angry or out of touch anymore, but she still wasn't herself. She acquired a twitch in her right eye and a tremor in her left hand. My heart ached for her. The doctor told us the medicine caused the side effects, but was optimistic she would get over them quickly.

"Give it time," the doctor said. "It should pass."

CeCe made most of the trips to the hospital alone. They only had afternoon and evening visits. We couldn't keep leaving school early, and CeCe didn't like driving there at night. When she did visit, she spoke to the doctor regularly and updated Luke and me. Mama had sick leave benefits, and CeCe brought Mama's paycheck for her to sign each week so we'd continue to have money for food and bills. Luke and I went about our lives like usual, and forced ourselves to call Mama once a day. I can't speak for Luke, but it felt awkward talking to her while she was there. What could I talk about? I certainly didn't want to share what was going on in my life, and I feared what might be going on in hers.

On the way back from one of her visits, CeCe came home wearing Mama's white rabbit jacket with the hood and an armful of groceries. Her long brown hair shining with eggplant highlights fell to one side. Her eyelashes were thick and longer than ever. She looked alive again - not pale and drained as she had been. Maybe she had a secret boyfriend, I thought.

"Luke, go get the rest of the bags out of my trunk," she ordered. "We need to brighten this place up. Fill it with some holiday cheer."

She placed the bag on the kitchen table and started unpacking. "I've got cookie mix and eggnog." She handed me the eggnog and pointed toward the refrigerator. "Olivia, I'll need your help too."

I smirked. "Help with what?"

"Decorations!" she said. "It won't feel like Christmas without decorations." She pointed to the back door. "Go in the shed and get out the box."

It didn't feel like Christmas at all. I couldn't imagine how it would, regardless of any decorations, but I complied with CeCe's request anyway. Rummaging through the mess in the shed, I pulled out the box CeCe was talking about, brought it inside, and helped put out a few items on the end tables and kitchen countertops. We didn't have a tree, so there really wasn't much more we could do. Maybe decorating took CeCe's mind off Mama, but it did nothing for me. I didn't take pleasure in any of that stuff like CeCe and Mama did. Instead, I preferred to find the holiday spirit while spending it with my friends.

And that reminded me. I hadn't spoken to Matt in over a week. Neither of us had said it, but in my mind we'd broken up.

Although I still had feelings for him, I couldn't forgive him for cheating on me and acting like he did nothing wrong. Instead, I set my sights on Tuck Peterson.

CHAPTER 14

T uck was as different from Matt as Georgia was from New York City. Matt was dark-haired with a wiry build with biceps that made him appear larger than his physical stature. Six feet tall with blonde hair and blue eyes, Tuck's muscular body was created for football and females. It made up for the depth his personality lacked. Not my usual type, but his other attributes helped me overlook that.

Matt hated football players, and they hated him. Most southern girls liked the Yankee boys in our school, but southern boys did not. When Matt moved in, he found his place in school with other guys with similar backgrounds; however, his dark complexion and musical talent made him especially unpopular with Tuck.

Even worse, everyone assumed Matt lacked intelligence

because of his New York City accent and nonchalant attitude. In truth, he was smarter than Tuck *and* most of the football team. The previous year, our English teacher made that known in front of the entire class. Tuck became so angry, he and his buddies made it their mission to make Matt wish he was back in New York, but Matt always prevailed because of his NYC wit.

Tuck's parents had planned a party for his seventeenth birthday on December 20th. They invited all of his friends, including me. Most of his friends weren't mine, and I wasn't looking forward to going. Especially having to fraternize with Monica Bradshaw, whom I knew would be there. On top of that, I only had twenty dollars from the money CeCe gave me from Mama's check.

According to Dr. Foster and Mr. Shimmering, Mama would be coming home on December 22. I focused on Mama coming home and getting through the Christmas season. We still hadn't put up a tree or done any shopping, but CeCe assured us we'd get it all done before she came home.

But until then, I kept my mind on Tuck. He was crazy about me, which made being with him tolerable. Each year since seventh grade, Tuck had told me, "One day you're gonna be my girlfriend, Olivia." That always made me laugh. When I first met him, he was scrawny with buckteeth. The following summer he returned to school tall and muscular. However, his zit-covered face and his teeth wrapped in thick metal braces didn't entice me. Again, I passed.

This year he came back without the braces and even bigger muscles. When I saw him at the beginning of the school year, he grabbed me by the waist and hoisted me in the air like a barbell. "Hey Olivia, good to see you," he said, and grinned wide. His new smile and clear skin combined with his even larger muscles finally piqued my interest. This time when he asked me out, I agreed.

Now, I had to get Tuck a gift for his birthday, and I had procrastinated until the afternoon before his party. Jonzie agreed to take me to the mall. When she pulled up in front of the trailer she honked the horn as usual.

"Who's making that racket?" CeCe asked.

"It's Jonzie. We're going to the mall, remember?" I grabbed my purse and rushed out the door.

As soon as we pulled onto the main road, Jonzie turned down the radio. "What are you gonna get him?"

"I don't know, maybe I'll get him a shirt or a cassette tape . . . I have no idea." I turned the radio back up. "I love this song." The Chipmunk's Christmas song played.

She shook her head. "Why are you going out with him

anyway? You and Tuck have nothing in common. He's a big dumb jock. I don't get you."

"He's not that dumb," I said. "He's crazy about me and he's got huge biceps."

"Oh, my… you are missing the point, girl. I thought you were the smart one!"

I felt it was good for me to go out with someone different than Matt. Tuck didn't have what Matt had - the thing that made me feel I didn't deserve him. I wanted to be in control of my feelings this time. With Matt, I felt my only known identity was as Matt's girlfriend. It wasn't that way with Tuck. I just wasn't so sure that I wanted Tuck to be the first one to take me *water-skiing*, and that seemed to be the goal of everyone I knew this year, except maybe Bessa.

"What you are really saying is, Tuck is a BTN."

"What's a BTN?"

"Oh, come on," she nudged. "Better than nothing!"

I looked away and turned the radio back up. Jonzie turned it back down. I didn't want her to know the way I really felt, not about everything at least. So I said, "What's wrong with going out with him until someone better comes along?"

She smiled. "That's what I thought."

I didn't see any harm in it. No one wanted to be dateless

during the holidays. Jonzie would expect an answer like that from me, rather than the mere fact that I needed to feel superior for once and not alone. After Daddy died and we moved to Stargazer Court, people treated me differently. It didn't make sense, and it wasn't fair, and I was tired of it. Jonzie and Tuck already thought I was cool, and I needed that feeling desperately.

We arrived at the mall at 4:00. I had to be at Tuck's house by 7:00.

Dodging last-minute shoppers, we squeezed through the crowds. Good-looking guys roamed the mall in droves, and I couldn't keep my eyes from following them.

For the first time in awhile, I felt good about myself. Having a hunky boyfriend was overrated. Having to be on guard for boyfriend snatchers wore me out. Only now, I lumped myself in with the girls I despised. I couldn't keep my eyes in their sockets, and they zoomed right to the backside of a guy who resembled Matt, but with shorter hair. I moved in closer. He turned around.

"Well, look who's here."

His crooked smile had more power over me than my curling iron. My anger disappeared, and all I saw was the gorgeous hunk who made my heart rock.

"Hey, what's up?"

Jonzie kicked my ankle. For the next few moments, she didn't exist. I pretended that Tuck didn't either. When I realized Jonzie was still standing there, I whispered in her ear, "Don't be mad at me, but I'm going to hang out with Matt."

She shouted a whisper back. "I guess I'll shop by myself, even though I came here for *you*." I knew I was wrong and being stupid, but I couldn't help myself. Matt grabbed my hand and we took off. I followed him to his car in the parking lot. Perhaps all my bottled-up feelings about Mama, and thinking about my future and fearing CeCe leaving, led me to behave in a manner unlike myself. Matt and I made out in his car like we'd never been apart. The steamy windows closed us off from the world, as well as my good judgment.

When I checked back into reality, I realized what I didn't do and what I did do: shop for Tuck's present and cheat on him with Matt. I thought Matt and I were finished. Now, I wasn't sure. Before I could go on any further with the relationship, I needed to know why Matt cheated on me. So, I finally asked.

"Who was that girl you were with the night I came to your house?" I folded my arms over my pounding heart and waited for an answer.

"I tried to tell you, but you wouldn't listen," he said. "Then I got mad at you for not wanting to hear me out."

My heart raced harder at the memory. "I'm listening now. Go ahead. Who was she? And why were you with her when I thought we were exclusive?"

"She's my cousin."

I pushed him away. "So, you're a full-fledged redneck now, messing 'round with your cousin? Eww!"

He chuckled. "I may live here, but I'm still a New Yorker. There'll be no missing limbs from my family tree."

I turned away, still angry. "Then why was your shirt off?"

He unbuttoned his shirt and held his left arm out. "Pull."

I hesitated.

"Go ahead, pull."

I tugged his shirtsleeve and exposed his shoulder. A heart-shaped tattoo with a rose wrapped around it appeared . . . with my name written inside. My name! I was in awe and angry at the same time—angry at myself for never hearing Matt out—angry I was supposed to be with Tuck, but wanted to be with Matt.

"My cousin is a tattoo artist," he said. "She was just goofing around when you came to the door."

It took a minute, but finally, I was able to say, "Why didn't you tell me?"

"I wanted to surprise you but then you started acting all weird. You didn't call me back, you avoided me at school, and then you started going out with Tuck." Matt shook his head back and forth in disgust the whole time he listed all that I'd done to him, ending by saying, "All after I had *your* name inked on my arm. So who got surprised, huh?"

I slumped down in the seat. "I'm *surprised*, all right."

"You don't like it?"

"It's the coolest thing anyone's ever done for me," I said, and I wrapped my arms around him.

"You know," he said. "My cousin's coming back to fix it."

"What do you mean?"

He cocked his head to the side and stared at me. "She's gonna make a design over your name."

I didn't want Matt to cover up my name. Just thinking about it made my stomach hurt, but right before I began making out with him again, I checked my watch and realized how late I was for Tuck's party. My mind went blank and I couldn't respond to what he just told me. All I could do was try to find a way to tell Matt that I had to go to Tuck's party. Guilt ate at me like fire ants on a dead possum. I wanted to be with Matt worse than ever, but I couldn't break up with Tuck on his birthday. I thought about how I'd feel if someone did that to me. I just couldn't do it, as much as I wanted to.

Finally, at 9:00, I said, "I don't know how to say this, but . .

. have to go. And I need a ride."

"Why?" he said, already reaching for the ignition. "Where do you have to go?"

"Tuck's house. It's his birthday and his parents are throwing him a party."

His hand grasped the key and froze. His face transformed into an emotionless imposter of himself. "You're not serious?"

My voice began to crack. I tried not to cry. "I don't want to go, but I can't stand him up on his birthday. I just can't be that mean."

"To him! What about me?" He let go of the key and banged his fist on the dashboard. "I can't believe you."

"I didn't expect to see you today. I didn't expect any of this to happen." I peered down and picked at my right eyelash. Silence enveloped the moment.

"Say something."

"I didn't expect to see you either, but I did," he said. "Doesn't that mean anything to you?"

He stared straight, avoiding my eyes. I would've been just as angry. It was plain crazy asking him to do drive me to Tuck's house.

"I'm sorry," I said. "I'm gonna break up with him, just not tonight," I pleaded.

He didn't say another word. He turned on the ignition and drove out of the parking lot. We drove for ten minutes without saying one word to each other. When we turned down the street before Tuck's house, I said, "Stop here."

I didn't want anyone to see me get out of his car.

He stopped the car short and I jolted forward. "So what was tonight?" he asked.

"It was everything!" I reached over and put my hand on his leg. He pushed it off. "I'll break up with Tuck tomorrow, I promise."

He turned toward me, his dark eyes like shells ready to eject from a two-barrel shotgun. "Tomorrow's too late."

My heart stopped, and I couldn't breathe. Five minutes ago, I was in heaven. Now I was trapped in purgatory. I closed my eyes to keep the tears from falling and opened the door and got out of the car. I took a deep breath and said, "I'll call you," but he didn't answer or look at me. I shut the door - he drove away.

I walked down the block praying I had inherited one ounce of CeCe's acting ability, because I was about to put on my first big show.

CHAPTER 15

"Where the heck have you been?"

I didn't answer at first when Tuck opened the front door and threw words at me like rocks from a slingshot. While I dug into my personal bank of lies for a believable story, he pulled me inside by the arm and slammed the door shut. It suddenly dawned on me that I hadn't bought him a gift. In that instant, the lie came, and the flow of tears streamed down my face.

"What's the matter?" he asked.

"I . . . I . . . I got you a present at the mall, then we stopped to get a bite to eat and I left your gift on the seat. When I went back to look for it, it was gone. I thought maybe I left it in the dressing room of another store and went back there. I spent all night scouring the mall trying to find your gift, but I never did."

He wrapped his arms around me. "I'm sorry, it's okay. I'm just glad you're here."

I felt cheap and fake. The tears I shed were real, but they belonged to Matt, not Tuck. Now I understood how CeCe felt after she had Luke steal Mama's car. Lies are like snowballs with rocks inside. You can form them into any size or shape you want, but the liar always knows about the extra weight they carry.

The faint smell of Matt's Aramis remained on my clothes, and for an instant, I pretended it was Matt holding me.

* * *

Monday morning, I went to my locker and found a yellow sticky note on the door.

I know what you did, Spelling Slut.

I crumpled the note and shoved it into my pocket. Bessa popped up beside me.

"How was the party?" She stared into my eyes, as if she expected to gain a little experience through my stories.

"Nothing special," I said, and turned my head to avoid her gaze.

"So what did you get him for a present? I hope you wrapped it good and not with duct tape." She giggled.

I bent down and picked up my math book. I wanted to get to class and forget about the whole night.

Bessa waved her hand in front of my face. "Hell-*o*, is anyone in there? I feel like I'm having this conversation with myself. What's going on?"

I slammed my locker door shut.

Jonzie popped up behind us both. "How'd it turn out?"

Bessa put her hands on her hips. "Do you know something I don't? Because Miss Olivia is being all tight-lipped and won't share anything with me."

Jonzie and Bessa both glared at me, waiting for answers.

"It's too much to tell right now. We'll talk during lunch period," I said. "But let's skip and meet in the parking lot."

"Fine with me," Jonzie said. "I spent my lunch money on lipstick."

Bessa pinched the skin from her side. "Fine with me too. I ate too much this weekend."

The bell rang. We separated and went to our classes. At noon the three of us met by Bessa's car and climbed inside. Bessa sat in the driver's seat, I took the passenger's seat, and Jonzie sat on the back of the console. Bessa started the car so we'd have heat. Jonzie pulled the rearview mirror in her direction and reapplied her lipstick.

Bessa started cleaning out her pocketbook. "Who wants to go see *Nightmare on Elm Street* with me Friday night?" she asked.

"You've seen it five times already!" Jonzie proclaimed.

Bessa flashed a sheepish grin. "I might as well tell you."

"Tell us what?" Jonzie and I asked simultaneously.

"I'm saving myself for Johnny Depp." She giggled.

Jonzie smirked. "You already told us that, and I still don't even know which one he is."

Bessa placed her hand over her heart. "He's the most perfect-looking guy in the movie . . . in the world! You can't miss him. I know he'll be famous one day, and I'll be waiting."

"You're too sheltered," Jonzie said. "I'm surprised your granny even lets you go to the movies."

Bessa turned away and stuffed the garbage from her purse into the trash bag hanging from the radio knob. "Oh stifle it, Jonzie." She flicked her hand as to shoo her away. "It isn't a sin to fantasize!" She blushed. "Enough about me—spill, Olivia."

Jonzie kissed the top of her hand to remove her excess lipstick. Still holding the trash bag, Bessa turned toward me. Now both she and Jonzie sat gaping, waiting to hear the dirt. I covered my mouth and secretly grinned. I found it humorous how badly they wanted to know what was going on in my social life. Actually, I don't think my life had ever been livelier, or should I say filled with drama.

"I'll tell you what happened," Jonzie said. "Then maybe Olivia will fill us in on the rest. First, Miss Livy saw Matt in the mall after asking me to drive her there so she could buy Tuck a birthday present. Not ten minutes later, she dumped me and took off with Matt, but she was supposed to be at Tuck's party at 7:00. I don't even know if she went. Did you go?"

Bessa held onto her garbage with white knuckles and stared at me. "I thought you said you went. Did you?"

I took a deep breath. "Well . . . yes."

Jonzie's eyes widened. Bessa gazed toward heaven and shook her head.

"What was I supposed to do, it was his birthday!" I brought my knees to my chest and hugged them.

"So what!" Jonzie said. "It's not like he's five years old. Matt's the one you want, right?"

"Yeah," I said, but my euphoric moment faded quickly.

"So, what happened with Matt?" Jonzie asked again.

"Matt and I hung out in his car for two hours. Everything was going great. He didn't cheat on me by the way. The girl at his house that night was his cousin."

"Ewww," Jonzie and Bessa groaned.

"It wasn't like that, it was a misunderstanding on my part. Anyway, I thought we were getting back together. He even got a tattoo on his shoulder with my name on it."

"A tattoo!" Jonzie exclaimed.

"Yup, it's beautiful. Everything was so perfect until I realized I had to get to Tuck's party."

"What did you do?" Bessa asked.

"What else could I do? I asked Matt to drop me off at Tuck's house—only I made him drop me off a block away."

"You're ruthless," Bessa said.

Jonzie nodded in agreement.

I shot them both a narrow stare. "You would have done the same thing. It was his birthday. I guess the two of you don't have as much of a conscience as I thought." I smirked. "Anyhow, even though he dropped me off a block away, someone must have seen me because I found this note on my locker." I pulled it from my pocket and held it open.

"*Spelling Slut!* What the heck does that mean?" Jonzie asked.

"It must have come from someone who knew me in middle school. It's got to be one of those cheerleaders." I rolled my eyes. "Back in middle school I was a bit of a nerd. Also a wannabe cheerleader. I made friends with a few cheerleaders. I also entered all the spelling bee contests too."

"Your life has more twists and turns than my soap opera,"

Jonzie said wide-eyed.

Bessa zipped up her now-tidy handbag. "I remember how good you were in spelling. It must have been one of them."

"Yup. Probably a jealous cacographer."

"Huh?" Both Jonzie and Bessa responded.

Bessa said, "What the heck is a caco . . .?"

"That was one of my spelling bee words way back when," I said. "It means a person who can't spell."

"Gee, I never thought of myself as a cacographer," Bessa said. "It sounds intelligent."

"Ahem," Jonzie cleared her throat. "Can we get back to the subject? Did you and Matt do it or what?"

"Is that all you think about?" I blurted. "No! We didn't do it! For goodness sake, I feel like a tramp as it is."

"So why did you get that note?" Bessa asked.

Wide-eyed and impatient, they both glared at me, waiting for an answer.

"Whoever saw me get out of Matt's car must have also been at Tuck's party."

Jonzie chuckled. "Do you have any idea which cacographer it might have been?" She asked sarcastically, while shoving her big glossy lips in my face.

"It had to be Monica, I just know it. She arrived at the party a couple of minutes after me."

"What are you gonna do?" Bessa asked.

There were many things I would have liked to do to Monica, but I didn't need any more problems at the moment.

"Nothing right now," I said. "But as the saying goes, 'What comes around goes around' and for now, I'll just watch and wait."

* * *

CeCe picked Luke and me up from school early and took us to K-mart. We zipped up and down the aisles filling the cart with items for Christmas. We found Mama a new outfit. Luke picked out a fake tree, garland, and something called "Christmas Tree in a Can," which was supposed to trick the nose into believing our tree was real. CeCe grabbed a poinsettia plant as well as a bunch of ingredients to make a sweet potato pie, and some small gifts like socks, gloves, magazines and a Clint Black CD to put under the tree for Mama. I was tempted to purchase a pair of fake eyelashes to enhance mine, which were thinning more and more each day, but I feared I'd look worse instead of better. We packed the car and drove toward home.

As soon as we got in the house, CeCe turned the radio on. While Nat King Cole sang about chestnuts roasting and Jack Frost, we began to complete the decorating for Mama's homecoming.

"Here Luke." CeCe handed him the base for the tree. "Loosen the screws so I can drop it inside."

Luke obeyed, and then helped CeCe wiggle the tree into the stand.

"Olivia, go get the ornaments." CeCe said.

I handed her the box and she reached inside and pulled out a drummer boy figurine.

"Luke, come help us decorate." CeCe handed him the figurine. "Daddy bought this the year you were born," she said.

I found the angel I had made from pipe cleaners in second grade and hung it up, and CeCe put some candy canes on the branches. Together the three of us decorated the tree with everything we could find in the box.

"Step back," CeCe said and sprayed the tree with Christmas-Tree-in-a-Can, and then plugged in the lights. The sounds and scents of Christmastime filled our home making it seem like there might be a possibility we could find joy this Christmas after all.

"How's Mama doing?" I asked. "I didn't call her yesterday." It was hard to make conversation with her. She was so quiet, and I didn't really want to discuss all that had been going on in my life. "Are the side effects going away yet?"

"She's not shaking as much as before, and the tremors have gone away," CeCe said. "I spoke to the doctor and he said she's responding well to the medicine, though it makes her tired and she's not quite used to it yet."

Luke's eyebrows bunched together and he stared at CeCe nervously.

"Don't worry. Everything's gonna be fine." Then she said, "Let's clean this place up. Whose turn is it to vacuum the floor? Luke, get those bicycle parts off your bed and change your sheets. Olivia, if your clothes pile any higher in the hamper, they're gonna touch the ceiling."

She wasn't exaggerating much. I *had* been slacking on cleaning since Mama had been gone. I saluted her. "Yes, Ma'am—right away."

She shot us a beady-eyed grin and waved. "Go on, get moving."

I grabbed a load of laundry and tossed it in the washing machine, then cleaned off my dresser. I checked in on Luke and saw him shove his bicycle parts under the bed. Luke *always* slacked off when it came to cleaning. When I went to help in the kitchen, CeCe had already mopped the floor and did the dishes. The place never looked so good. Finally, we were ready to pick up Mama.

"Do I have to come?" Luke asked.

"Of course," CeCe said. "Mama wants to see all of us, so rid yourself of that attitude."

He hung his head and didn't reply.

Once again we headed back to Milledgeville. The hairs on my arms stood up the moment we entered the gates. When we passed those awful gravesites, I actually shivered. But maybe it wasn't just the memories. Although we were happy Mama would be coming home, it felt strange after so many weeks with her away.

As soon as we entered the hospital, I spotted the same woman I'd met the first time we'd gone there. The one who kept talking to me. I remembered her odd name - Minta. She appeared much different from the last time I'd seen her. She wore a pair of cranberry colored pants and a winter white jacket. Her hair, a brighter shade of white with a tinge of blue blended well with her earrings. Sapphires. They flashed when the sunlight beaming through the window caught their attention.

Minta moved toward me. "I know you. Are you here to see me? I'm going home today." She grinned. The faraway gaze in her eyes still lingered, but it seemed closer than before.

"I'm here to pick up my mother," I said.

She straightened up, seeming taller than I remembered her.

"And who might your mother be?"

"Cassandra Travis."

She broke into another big smile. "I know Cassandra. We sat next to each other during Arts and Crafts. She made the loveliest wooden butterfly, painted it pink and yellow. My name is Minta. Minta Gray."

Arts and Crafts! What kind of place is this? I thought. *We sent Mama here to get her mind fixed, not prepare her to open a craft store!*

"We spent a lot of time together. She told me she had beautiful children. Please tell your mama to call me some time. I'd like to take her shopping. I gave her my phone number." She smiled again. "She reminds me of my daughter. They would've liked each other."

Minta's big-toothed grin closed to a solemn smile. And I was surprised to realize I liked her, in a strange way.

"Yes, Ma'am. I will," I told her.

A man about Mama's age appeared beside her. "Good luck, y'all, and Merry Christmas!" Minta said, and waved. She hung from his arm like a Christmas ornament while they strolled out the door.

A minute later, Mama sauntered down the hallway and entered the lobby. Her hair was shorter, cut into a bob. She looked more sophisticated than she could ever be. She smiled with her usual closed lips.

"Mama, look at your hair!" CeCe ran her hand down the side of Mama's head.

"Do you like it?" she said. "It's not really me. But it was free and all. One of the nurses cut it—she told me she was a hairdresser before she became a nurse."

CeCe kissed her cheek. "It's good to change your hairdo once in a while. It makes you feel like a new person."

I secretly hoped she *was* a new person. A sane person. I also wondered how safe it was to have a nurse visiting patients with scissors in their hands.

Mama's eyes found mine. "Hi, Olivia, aren't ya gonna give me a hug? You too, Luke."

Luke and I hugged Mama from each side. I'd been unsure of what to expect, but she seemed like the Mama we knew before the breakdown, even cheerful again. She was dressed in the clothes CeCe bought for her - a green fleece sweat outfit with matching slippers. But I found it hard to relax after all that had happened.

Mr. Shimmering appeared, and we followed him to his paper-infested office.

"Sit down, please," he said, pointing to the chairs.

He pulled two pill bottles from his pocket and placed them on top of his desk. "This is the medication the doctor prescribed for Cassandra." He spoke the words as if Mama wasn't there. He picked one bottle up and held it at eye level. "This is Stelazine. It seems to be working well. However, we will need to check Cassandra's blood levels in a few weeks to see if it's still a good match for her. Side effects may continue to occur, and she might be tempted to stop her medication. If this happens, she needs to see the doctor immediately."

He picked up the other bottle. "This is a tranquilizer called Ativan. Cassandra should take one Stelazine pill each day. The Ativan is only for the times she feels extra stress and agitation."

Finally, he turned to meet Mama's eyes. "It will help you calm down. And don't forget to drink a lot of water too."

He turned back toward CeCe and me. "This is not a cure," he said in a deeper tone of voice. "There is no cure, only medication to help Cassandra remain functional. There are refills available for both. She may need to try several medications before we find one that's best for her."

He handed me a business card and gave one to Mama. "This is the name of a doctor in your area. You need to make an appointment with him for your next refill."

He stood up, offered his hand to Mama, and then CeCe.

"Good luck."

We shuffled out of his office, ready to begin a new life with Mama. One without the craziness, I hoped.

I held my hand out. "Here, let me take that for you."

She sat in the front seat of the car and was quiet the first few miles. Shortly after that, she blurted, "That Shimmering has more patients to handle than I have hairs on my head. He can't keep 'em straight. How can I trust he gave me the right medicine?"

"I spoke with your doctor ahead of time," CeCe said. "Don't worry. He gave you the right medicine."

Mama's tone changed. "I don't ever want to go to that place again. Do you understand?" She scowled. "There's nothing but crazy people in there. All except Minta and me. We're not like the others. They've all got problems with drugs and drinking. Big deal, so I get confused sometimes. That doesn't make me crazy. What makes me crazy is this ringing in my ears and being thirsty all the time from that stinking medicine."

"Don't worry, Mama. The side effects will stop," CeCe replied, keeping her eyes on the road. "The doctor told me so. And I've already seen most of them fading. You just have to stick it out. Maybe you should take the other medicine to help you relax. You've been through a lot."

"Yeah," I added. "You've been through a lot."

I could see CeCe in the rearview mirror, but I couldn't see Mama's expression so I couldn't be sure what else might be going on in her mind. But I had a sinking feeling.

Luke fell asleep as usual. Mama went back to being quiet while CeCe drove. I stared out the window at the homes covered in Christmas lights. I wondered what the New Year and the *new* Mama would bring.

CHAPTER 16

My job at home was to check the mail, and the last few days I'd forgotten. The mailbox was stuffed, and I grabbed the mail, sat down at the kitchen table and ripped open anything that resembled a card or letter. Sure enough, I found a card with Aunt Nadine wearing a Santa hat and bright red lipstick, along with a two-hundred-dollar check. Surprisingly, Grandma and Grandpa actually placed a check in their card this year. The other cards were from Bessa's granny, and Jonzie, and one I didn't recognize. I opened it and read:

> *Dear Cassandra and Kids,*
>   *Belinda and I are moving to Jacksonville and would like to come for a visit. I know it's been a long time, but family shouldn't remain separated. We'll be moving down this spring. I hope you'll be happy to see us.*

Love,
Bradley

He even included a check for one hundred dollars. "Hmmm," I muttered, grinning, "I like you already, Uncle Bradley."

We hadn't seen Uncle Bradley since Daddy's funeral. We hadn't seen anyone from Daddy's family since the funeral. Actually, we'd barely seen anyone from Daddy's family even before the funeral. Whenever I tried to talk about that with Mama, she turned cold and silent. Knowing I had family members in the greatest city in the world, with whom I had no contact, was a mystery I hoped to unravel one day. After receiving this letter, maybe now I would.

Well, *I* was excited to see him. I hoped Mama would be too.

"Mama, CeCe, Luke, we got a special card in the mail," I shouted, and put the checks in a separate pile.

They all gathered around me. "Who's it from?" CeCe asked first and picked up the card.

"Uncle Bradley," I answered, curious to hear Mama's response.

"Let me see that." Mama grabbed the card from CeCe's hand and read it. "Why, after all these years, does he want to see us?"

"He says right here." I pointed to the place on the card and said it aloud. "Family shouldn't remain separated."

"Hmmm," was all Mama said.

Luke practically jumped out of his sneakers. "I've got an uncle?"

"I guess you wouldn't remember him," CeCe said. "You only met him once, at Daddy's funeral."

"This is so cool," he said, and smiled in a way I hadn't seen him do in ages.

It was good to see him smile.

Mama, still overly calm, caused *me* anxiety. I tried to distract her by saying, "Don't you think we should go to church tonight?"

CeCe shot me an evil eye. I suppose, after sacrificing the turkey because of our sinful souls, she feared church might not be the best place to bring Mama. But we'd always gone to Landon Baptist Church on Christmas Eve. And before Daddy died, we went every Sunday. I missed going. The church people were the closest thing we'd ever had to a family.

"No, I'd like to just stay in tonight," Mama said.

"Okay, Mama, whatever you want," I replied, and hung the Christmas cards with tape from the top of the doorway to the kitchen.

* * *

The next day was quiet, with no visitors. We opened the wrapped gifts from K-mart with each of our names on it. Grandma and Grandpa called to wish us a Merry Christmas, and acted as if Mama had never been gone for weeks at a mental hospital. CeCe helped Mama bake a ham and some collard greens and mashed potatoes, and I made the cornbread we always had. For dessert, we had sweet potato pie and drank eggnog while we watched *It's a Wonderful Life*. Christmas passed us by without an inch of excitement except for the anticipation that in a few months, we'd be meeting our uncle. And except for Mama's mentioning of the name Westin Barnes.

* * *

After New Year's Day, Mama returned to work at the nursing home. CeCe went back to the community college and cleaning houses, and Luke and I went to school as before.

Tuck found out about my night with Matt before I had a chance to break up with him. Matt couldn't forgive me for ditching him. Probably to get back at me, Tuck began dating Monica, and even though I was one of the few remaining virgins in my junior class, I became known as the Spelling Slut of Landon High.

Sick of the rumors, I decided not to date any more high school boys. Jonzie and I paid her cousin ten dollars to make us fake IDs so we could seek out more mature-minded males. Our plan was to hang out at the Hunka Bunka Ballroom on the edge of town. It was a rock club, not a ballroom anymore, but for some odd reason the owner never changed the name. Probably cost too much money to buy a new sign.

"Bessa, you have to come with us," I said. "Jonzie's cousin'll make you an ID too."

"Are you crazy?" she said. "My granny would never let me stay out that late. Besides, being in a smoky bar isn't good for my voice," she reminded me. "I have to sing in church on Sunday and you know I'm not into going to that sort of place."

"Yeah, I know. Just thought I'd ask." Not for a moment did I think she'd say yes. Maybe I even wanted her to tell me I shouldn't go, just like she was always telling me things I shouldn't do.

On a Saturday night in late January, Jonzie and I hit our first rock and roll club. I told Mama I'd be babysitting with Jonzie, and she told her mama she'd be babysitting with me. Even though she rarely paid much attention to where I went, I made up the story anyway, just in case the medicine caused that to change.

We stood in line outside the door, shivering from the cold. Neither of us wore our coats since we didn't want to cover up our new outfits.

Mine wasn't really new. I'd lost those five extra pounds and snuck out wearing CeCe's new jeans and her black cashmere sweater, which slightly exposed my right shoulder. I even borrowed her hoop earrings.

Jonzie wore a pink hooded sweater with a white star across the chest and a pair of black pants that laced up the front. Her spiked-heel boots lifted her about six inches off the ground. Even though I had heels on too, Jonzie still made me look short.

The band played so loudly the music rumbled inside my chest. "Give me some lipstick," Jonzie hollered in my ear. It was her fifth application in ten minutes.

My pointy-toed boots started to cut off the circulation to my toes. I wanted to get inside and sit down.

"The line's moving. Quick, get your ID out," Jonzie said, and shoved me ahead.

I rummaged through my purse and pulled it out. It appeared authentic to me, but I didn't know if it would go over with the guy at the door.

"I'm nervous," I whispered to her.

"Shhhhh, play it cool."

Jonzie went first. A burly guy with a band t-shirt, ripped up black jeans and a feather earring in his ear checked her ID. He stared into her eyes and cocked his head toward the door. "Go on in."

Jonzie wandered in and headed toward the bar. Although taller and plastered with makeup, I figured my over-developed chest would draw attention from my baby face and I'd follow her right in. The guy checked me out and examined my ID. He asked what year I was born.

"1961," I said, pretending to sound annoyed.

"You look young for your age," he commented.

I smiled. "I guess that means I'll look young when I'm old."

He handed back my ID. "Go ahead." He waved on the next person in line.

Jonzie and I bolted straight to the bathroom, grabbed each other's hands, jumped up and down and chanted in high-pitched whispers, "We're in, we're in, we're in!"

"Let's get a drink," she suggested.

We made our way to the crowded bar. I edged myself in between two guys. I stretched out my arm and waved a five-dollar bill in the air.

The bartender slapped down two napkins. "What can I get

ya?"

"Two Cokes," I hollered above the music.

I felt a pinch in the back of my arm. I turned around. Jonzie pushed herself in front of me and shouted, "Make that rum and Cokes."

The memory of spewing all over Matt's living room floor remained fresh in my mind. I didn't intend to finish the drink, but like a fool, I did anyway. At least I stopped after two this time. Wide-eyed and filled with excitement that we pulled it off, I gazed around the smoky bar, and Landon seemed a million miles away. It reminded me how desperate I was to get away for real.

Two girls in the seats to the right of us got up. Jonzie and I snagged them before anyone else could, and scoped the place out with fascination. Jonzie jabbed me in the arm. "Hot guy at two o'clock." I swiveled myself around on the barstool and checked him out. A Bon Jovi look-alike stood beneath recessed lights with a halo of smoke surrounding his head.

"He winked at me," Jonzie said.

"Wink back."

I couldn't believe I was telling Jonzie what to do. She'd always been more aggressive than me in every way, especially guys.

She smiled at the guy. Then sounding panicked, she said,

"He's coming over."

She sat up straight, shook her head, and loosened her bangs in front of her face. The closer he got to us, the less I thought he resembled Jon. *Too bad.*

The guy walked over. "Hey," was all he said.

"Hey," she said back.

"What's your name?"

"I'm Jonzie and this is Olivia," she wrapped her arm around my neck.

"What ya drinkin'?" he asked.

"Rum and Coke."

He threw a twenty on the bar, and the bartender came over and he ordered Jonzie and me another one. Within a few minutes Jonzie disappeared, so I did a little room-surfing myself, catching glimpses of each good-looking guy and skipping the rest. I felt warm and tingly again, just like I had the night of the concert. An abstract painting of dancing drunks floated on the dance floor.

My eyes stopped dead center at one who reminded me of Matt. I smiled. He smiled back. Then he promenaded over to my seat. We exchanged names, and before I knew it, Tom offered me another drink, and he and I were lip-locked in the corner of the bar. Jonzie was nowhere to be found.

"You wanna take a ride? He asked. "I have to pick up

some money from a friend."

I hesitated. "Is it far?"

He scratched the tip of his nose. "No. Just a few miles down the road."

Leaving with this guy wasn't the smartest thing to do, but after my third rum and Coke, my decision-making skills had gone down the toilet. "All right, Tom, but I don't usually get in cars with strangers."

He grinned in a playful-sadistic way. "I'm not a stranger. I'm your new best friend."

"Let me tell my *other* best friend what I'm doing." I said, and scanned the bar for Jonzie. I didn't see her anywhere. Since Tom said we wouldn't be long - and the alcohol had stifled my intelligence - I went along.

* * *

As I walked past the sea of parked cars, I detected motion in one. I recognized a very familiar red-robin tattoo. Squinting, I noticed the words "free bird" under it. In addition to her double-ended burning candle, Jonzie had added the red robin after she served six months under house arrest enforced by her parents for getting caught stealing lipstick from K-mart.

I knocked on the window. She pulled the back of her shirt down. "What's up?"

165

"I'm going for a quick ride, I'll be right back," I said.

She smiled and waved me on.

Tom and I walked past a few rows of cars and stopped in front of a blue Jeep. He opened the car door and got in first then leaned over and pulled the lock up for me; I slid inside.

"You sure we won't be long?" I asked him again.

He started the engine and laid his hand on my thigh. "It won't take more than a few minutes. Just sit tight."

We pulled up to a dark street with a row of tiny one-story houses.

"I'll leave the car on so you'll have some music," he said, and slammed the door shut.

Rethinking my decision to go with Tom took firm hold of my paranoia. *No, I'm not gonna do this.* After a few more minutes, I started thinking about my future. Although I couldn't imagine being alone with Mama if CeCe left – again - I began to feel selfish about my plan. Nevertheless, the fear of taking over her position of head-of-household drove me to carry on. I needed to get to the library. A scholarship was the only opportunity for me at this point, and I had to start studying for the SAT's.

It felt like I'd been in the car much longer than five minutes. I glanced at the clock and saw it had been fifteen. My heart began to pound, and that unsettled feeling planted itself right in its favorite spot in the pit of my stomach. Crazy thoughts began to run through my head. Rattled by nervousness, the hole in my gut grew. *What if someone killed him and he's dead inside the house? Maybe it's a set-up and he and his friend are waiting for me to come to the door so they can rape me.*

Ten more minutes passed. I thought hard and realized I had two choices. The only thing left was to pick one. I had no idea what the consequences were to one choice, but the other might well land me in jail.

CHAPTER 17

Mama told me the queasy feeling that sits in your belly is God's way of speaking to you. A moment after I realized I had to make a choice, God spoke, so I listened, and I slid over to the driver's side of Tom's Jeep and drove away. I tried to remember the way back to the bar while following the speed limit so I wouldn't dare be pulled over. Now, both Luke and I were official car thieves.

Once I found the bar, I drove through the parking lot looking for Jonzie's car, but didn't see it. She must have figured I'd gotten a ride home from Tom. Why would she figure I'd do something so stupid? Maybe because I *was* stupid.

The threat of jail catapulted my heartbeat to an unnatural speed. I planned to ditch the car as soon as I got close enough to walk home. Luckily, landmarks I recognized helped me find my way home. McDonalds couldn't have appeared at a more perfect moment. Only two blocks from Stargazer Court, I pulled in and turned the lights and engine off. *What should I do with the keys? If I leave them in the ignition, someone might steal the car. Again. Maybe that's not a bad idea. What do I do?*

I felt that at any moment the police would arrive and arrest me. I started to think like a criminal and pulled a napkin from my purse, and wiped down the steering wheel to erase my fingerprints. After that, I lifted the floor mat, tossed the keys underneath, and took off on foot. My feet ached so bad I wanted to rip my spiked-heel boots off. If I'd had socks on, I probably would have, but my knee-highs would've ripped in a second. Exhausted and fearful, I reached the trailer and slithered inside using the backdoor. I climbed into bed and lay there begging God to let me sleep and forget about what I'd just done.

No sooner had I fallen asleep, the phone rang. I grabbed it before CeCe woke up.

"Where's my car?" the voice shouted.

Still half-asleep, I asked, "Who is this?"

"Don't mess with me, bitch! Where's my car? I can't

believe you stole my freakin' car. Are you crazy?"

Then I remembered, and I began to shake. More worried about leaving my fingerprints, I had given the creep my phone number.

Forcing my temper to remain intact and not wanting to wake CeCe I whispered, "I don't even know you . . . and you just left me there—"

"Just tell me where my car is," he shouted.

I told him, and he hung up. I thanked God I hadn't told him my last name or where I lived. I also thanked God for allowing me to get home safely and prayed that Jonzie got home safe too. I fluffed my pillow, which smelled like the smoke my hair had absorbed from the bar. I wondered if CeCe would smell it too. Still tipsy and too tired to think anymore, I fell asleep.

As soon as I woke up, I called Jonzie's house. Her mother answered and said she couldn't come to the phone. She didn't tell me why. I figured Jonzie had a hangover but at least I knew she was home.

That evening CeCe and I stayed in, but Luke went out. Mama had fallen asleep on the couch and we waited up for Luke to make sure he didn't wake her. Some time after midnight he walked through the door all glassy-eyed and smelling like smoke, but not like my hair had smelled the night before. Luke reeked of marijuana.

CeCe yanked him by the arm. In a loud whisper she said, "Mama's home now, Luke, you've got to quit acting up."

"Leave me alone, I'm goin' to bed." He spoke as if he were already sleeping. He kicked off his beat up work boots, causing them to roll across the living room floor, and trudged off to his bedroom.

"We've got to straighten him out," CeCe said as we watched him stumble down the narrow hallway. "He can't keep this attitude up. It'll land Mama back in the hospital in no time."

"If she ever wakes up," I said. "And besides, he's not gonna listen to us. We need someone else to talk to him."

She nodded. "Like help from a guy. Someone Luke will respect. He's done listening to women, but I can't think of anyone," CeCe said.

"Don't you have any male friends at college?" I asked, finding it hard to believe she didn't know anyone she could ask. CeCe never talked about guys anymore. Odd, since she was so popular with them in high school.

The last time she brought a guy home was during her senior year. Mama scared him away when she grilled him about politics. Mama's views were skewed. Not that *I* knew anything about politics; however, she said things that sounded almost . . .

communistic. Back then, I thought it was just Mama being bullheaded. Now I wondered if that was part of the sickness that had landed her in Central State.

Maybe CeCe likes older men and fears bringing them around Mama. That would make sense. *But why wouldn't she just tell me?* Definitely mysterious about the guy thing, I planned to find out why.

* * *

Sunday morning I called Jonzie's house again, but her mother still wouldn't let her talk. I worried something had happened to her Friday night. Or maybe her mom found out where she really went and grounded her. Different scenarios ran through my head. After stealing a car, I believed anything was possible.

At least Mama was more upbeat than usual, thanks to her medicine and having gone back to work. When suppertime rolled around, I yelled down the hallway. " Mama, are you fixing supper tonight?"

She didn't answer me. Instead, she sashayed into the living room and stopped between the couch and the loveseat. Her head held high, she flung her arms out and spun around. "What do you think?"

Dressed in a deep red v-neck dress that hugged her body

and stopped just past her knee, her bobbed hair twisted into a tight bun and face made up to perfection, she looked stunning.

"Wow, Mama," I managed. "You going somewhere?"

She grinned. Then she covered her mouth and giggled. "I'm going on a date."

She'd never gone on a date before—at least not since Daddy. There was that weird incident with the guy in the trailer who brought her home when she lost her car, but thank God, nothing had come of that. I couldn't imagine with whom or if she really did have a date at all.

"Who in the world do you have a date with?" I asked.

"Remember the nice man who drove me home when I lost my car?"

I jumped up from the couch. "Him? That man who took advantage of you!" After the other night, my faith in men had gone with the wind, and I didn't want Mama flying away too.

She tilted her head, all dreamy-eyed. "Olivia, he didn't take advantage of me, I took advantage of him."

It didn't sound right. How could she take advantage of him?

Just about the time CeCe heard us talking and joined in, the doorbell rang. I opened the door and there stood Westin Barnes.

He didn't resemble the memory I had of him at all. Neatly

groomed salt and pepper hair surrounded his peach colored face. His tie pressed and clipped and shiny brown shoes to match.

Mama ran to the door. "Come on in, Westin. Sit down." She dragged him by the hand to the couch. "Would you like a glass of sweet tea?"

He placed his hands in his lap like a little boy. "No thank you. We should be going. We don't want to be late for our reservations."

"Westin's taking me to Red Lobster." Mama smiled, sucking her lips inward. She strolled toward the closet and pulled out the long fox coat.

Red Lobster? I thought. *The closest thing Landon has to a fancy restaurant. This is serious!*

Westin jumped up and helped her slip on her coat. His gentlemanly behavior seemed sincere. Much more composed than the day he tried to sneak out the back like a thief in the night. Even so, CeCe and I glared at him as if to say, "You better not hurt our mama."

"Oh, I forgot my purse," she said. "I'll be right back."

As she headed down the hallway, Westin turned toward us with a smile and said, "How 'bout a joke? Everyone likes jokes, right?"

Luke's curiosity sparked, and he moseyed into the living

room from his spot at the kitchen table. "A joke? Watcha got?" he said.

We all sat down on the couch and eyeballed Westin.

"A man walks into a hamburger shop and orders a meal. The waitress brings his meal to him. He takes a bite out of it and notices there's a small hair in the hamburger. He begins yelling frantically at the waitress, 'Waitress, there's a hair in my hamburger! I demand to see what is going on!'

"So the waitress takes him back to where the cook is, and to his shock, he sees the cook take the meat patty and flatten it under his armpit. He says, 'That's disgusting!'

"Then the waitress says, 'You think that's disgusting, you should see him make donuts.'"

Luke grabbed his belly and howled with laughter. In between laughs, he said, "I gotta remember that one."

CeCe and I responded with a girly, "Eww!"

Westin breathed a small sigh of relief and grinned. "Don't worry, kids, I'll have your mama back before midnight." He winked just as Mama reappeared, and he opened the door and led her out, waving goodbye.

I didn't know what to make of the wink. It could have been innocent, or it could have been a con man's wink. I planned to watch Westin Barnes closely.

Mama turned back and said, "Don't wait up for me."

Luke jumped up and ran to the window, peeled the curtain back. "He's got a Cadillac. Maybe he's rich!"

"Maybe he's a car salesman and he borrowed the car," I said.

"Why are you being so cynical, Olivia?" CeCe said. "Mama hasn't been this happy in ages."

Luke let the curtain fall from his grip. "Maybe they'll bring me home a doggy bag."

CeCe and I rolled our eyes at Luke, and he boasted a goofy grin.

The phone rang and I lunged for it. Luke got there first. "It's for you," he said, wrinkling his nose in typical younger brother disgust. "It's Jonzie."

"Meet me at the park by the lake," she said. "Right away. My mama's out shopping and I'm grounded."

"Be there in fifteen minutes," I said, and hopped on Luke's bike because mine had a flat.

* * *

Jonzie sat waiting for me on our favorite bench when I arrived at the park, her back facing me. I jumped off the bike, flicked the kickstand down, and rushed to her.

She turned around, and I stopped cold. "Oh my gosh! What

happened to you?"

Jonzie sported a black eye and a fat lip.

"Remember the cute guy at two o'clock?"

I nodded, too stunned to speak.

She cocked her head to the right, showing me the rest of her bruises. "He turned out to be a zero."

"I . . . I saw you in the car. You seemed fine," I sputtered, trying to hold back my shock. That was impossible, though. Jonzie never seemed so fragile before.

She glanced away and with a scathing tone said, "Oh, he seemed nice at first."

"Don't they all," I interjected, sitting next to her. I thought about Mama and Westin, and how he seemed nice. Now I was more worried than ever.

"He moved too fast even for me." Jonzie re-focused her eyes toward her lap. "After I told him to slow down, he stopped being nice."

"He hit you because you said *no*?"

She raised her head. Her eyebrows were furrowed and her face red. "Not exactly. When he . . . when he wouldn't accept my *no*, I hit him!"

"You what?"

She nodded. "Maybe I led him on a little. But this guy was

a dog in heat. So I slapped him, and he hit me back. More than once. I don't know how I got away."

I leaned back on the bench, trying to absorb what she'd just said. "You're crazy, girl," I muttered. "We're both crazy."

She looked at me and said, "What happened to you?"

Seeing her eye bore into me through the bruises and swelling nearly made me cry - for her and for me. I told her my story, and what little color her face possessed seemed to vanish.

"YOU stole a car? I can't believe it. When I couldn't find you, I figured you were having fun and could take care of yourself."

"I thought the same about you." I couldn't help it. I laughed. Although risky, we both did take care of ourselves. We got out alive.

Jonzie smiled. "Ouch, don't make me laugh. It hurts."

"Well, isn't laughing better than crying?" I said, and elbowed her lightly in her side. "We better stick together from now on. I guess God doesn't want us in nightclubs."

"I don't know about God, but my mama sure doesn't!" Jonzie closed her eyes and nodded.

"You have your fake ID?" I asked.

Jonzie was wearing the same pants she had on the night we went out. She pulled it from her pocket. "Yeah, why?"

I put my hands on my hips and demanded, "Just hand it over."

She reluctantly placed it in my hand. "Maybe we're better off sticking with high school boys for now," she said, avoiding my eyes.

I shrugged and forced a chuckle. "Right now, I think I'll go it alone . . . at least for a little while." I put the IDs in my pocket and planned to cut them up when I got home. Although Jonzie said she had no future plans of going back to the bar, I still couldn't trust her with that power in her possession.

"Sure you don't want a cigarette?" she winked.

I rolled my eyes and gazed toward the sky. I drove home and remembered to pick up the mail on my way in. Mostly junk mail, except a letter with a New York return address. Uncle Bradley's.

I ripped the envelope open. He and his wife wanted to visit us the Saturday before Easter. When I showed Mama the card, she didn't respond in a good way. That's probably understating it. Actually, she yelled, "He's not coming to this house!"

I supposed she still harbored anger toward him for abandoning his duty as an uncle all these years. Even so, I saw no harm in his visit. "Mama, it'll be good for us to see family," I said.

"Especially Luke. He doesn't even know Uncle Bradley."

"You didn't seem to mind when he wrote us at Christmas," Luke added.

CeCe laid a hand on Mama's forearm.

"Mama, it'll be good for Luke—for all of us to meet someone related to Daddy."

Mama bit her bottom lip and fixed her eyes on the ceiling. "I suppose."

But she wouldn't make the call. In the end, CeCe called Uncle Bradley and told him we'd love to have him for a visit. A week later, he and his wife Belinda appeared outside our front door.

CHAPTER 18

Tall and handsome, Uncle Bradley resembled Daddy. He spoke with the same accent, dropping his *R's* at the end of words and adding them where they didn't belong.

Aunt Belinda seemed nice but didn't have much to say. Skinny, plain, and flat-chested, her main attraction seemed to be that she fluttered her eyelashes a lot. Not the way Mama did, more like she was trying to keep herself from sneezing.

The six of us squeezed in at the kitchen table and ate lunch - spaghetti and meatballs, one of the few meals Mama liked to cook. She said Daddy loved it, so Uncle Bradley would probably like it, too.

He told us a little about his job as an airplane mechanic and Luke ate up every word he said. Aunt Belinda continued to blink and nod while she listened and twirled spaghetti around her fork.

"Olivia, would you mind passing those delicious rolls?" he

asked, and leaned back in the chair as he rubbed his belly with the palm of his hand.

"Do you want some more *soder* too?" Luke asked, and cackled beneath his breath.

Uncle Bradley grinned the same way I remembered Daddy had. "Sorry, Luke, I meant pop or maybe some sweet tea." He said it with a pretend southern accent.

Luke giggled in a way I hadn't heard in years. "It's not pop, it's Coke," he said with a smile.

"I forgot you and your sisters are only half Yankee. I think you need to spend a little time with me and learn how the other half lives. What do you think about that, Luke?"

Luke turned toward Mama with hopeful eyes.

"I suppose." She sighed as her eyes darted back and forth, up and down. "Where do you plan on taking him?"

Uncle Bradley squirmed in his seat. "Actually, before we get settled in Jacksonville, Belinda and I figured we'd stop for a visit at Disney World. We thought maybe Luke would like to come with us."

"Disney World?" Luke jumped up from the table. "I've never been to Disney World!"

Uncle Bradley smiled. Belinda did too. "Does that mean you want to go?" he asked.

"Heck, yeah. I can go, right, Mama?"

"Right now I don't have enough room in the car to take you girls," he said. "But next time I'd like you to come for a visit too."

CeCe and I smiled. Mama's eyes continued flickering back and forth, not resting on any of us.

"I can go. *Right*, Mama?" he said louder.

CeCe jumped in. "Of course Mama will let you go. You have the entire week off from school." Her eyes dug into Mama, trying to get her to come back from wherever her mind had taken her.

Like she'd just heard the snap of fingers from a hypnotist, Mama said, "You'll have him back before school starts, right?"

Uncle Bradley sat straight in his seat. He seemed excited too. "Of course I will. The boy needs his education. Don't worry about a thing. We're gonna have a great time. Now go get packed, Luke. We need to be on the road soon."

I followed him to his room to help him gather his clothes together. He'd never gone away from home before, and I didn't want him to forget his underwear or socks. Luke beamed as he threw his clothes into the old suitcase, which not long ago had transported Mama's things back from the hospital. It was the only one in the house. I'm surprised it didn't bother him at the memory. I guess he was just too happy.

When Luke strolled into the living room carrying the suitcase, Uncle Bradley cringed. "Tell you what. Let's take a quick ride to K-mart. We'll get you a suitcase for a man, not an old lady."

"I beg to differ," Mama said. "I was a *young* lady when I bought that suitcase."

"Sorry, Cass, but to a young boy this is an old-lady suitcase."

Mama's eyes narrowed. "I suppose," she said.

Luke seemed to be holding his breath. Like if he moved or breathed, Uncle Bradley would change his mind. He wasn't accustomed to special treatment like this. When Uncle Bradley finally said, "Let's go," Luke grinned so wide, his cheeks looked like they were taped to his ears.

When they returned from the store, Luke not only had a new suitcase, but an entire new wardrobe. Uncle Bradley also brought CeCe and me a few items that Belinda must have picked out. I was surprised at how good it felt to be doted on. I felt a little envious of Luke, but in my heart I was happy for him. I'd forgotten that I'd prayed that God would find someone to help us with Luke. God answered my prayer, and I didn't even realize it until that instant.

Mama kissed Luke goodbye, and I noticed her whisper in Uncle Bradley's ear. I listened intently.

"Nothing better happen to my boy. He's Jimmy's son, and I'm not so sure he'd approve of you taking Luke, even to Disney."

He placed his arm on her back. "I can't change what's been done in the past, but I can make it right now. Please let me."

Luke interrupted. "I'm ready."

I shoved some candy in his pockets and tried not to cry when Uncle Bradley and Aunt Belinda drove him away in their black Mercedes while we waved goodbye.

* * *

I hadn't anticipated how empty the house would feel without Luke. Mama continued running off with Westin every chance she got. CeCe kept her business to herself, and for the first time in a long time, I didn't focus on anyone but me.

I relentlessly read textbooks during vacation. Determined to do well on the SATs, nothing else mattered to me except for obtaining a scholarship. If I managed to pull this off, Mama would be shocked, but thrilled. She couldn't deny me such an honor, regardless of her dreams for CeCe.

I hadn't really talked about my future before. CeCe was always the topic of our conversations when it came to the future.

We couldn't afford for me to go away to college anyway. I didn't want to go to the community college like CeCe. I dreamed of going somewhere prestigious like Princeton or Harvard, but mostly, somewhere far away from Landon. Anywhere.

Although CeCe planned to leave for Hollywood, she wouldn't expect me to give up a scholarship. Hollywood would still be there when I finished. That was my plan, the only way I could leave. I had every detail worked out. My guidance counselor would write a glowing letter of recommendation. And I needed to get involved with extra-curricular activities. Perhaps I could help out at a soup kitchen or a home for the elderly. The best place for me to start was the library. I hopped on Luke's bike.

When I got to the library, I hid the bike behind some shrubs. After brushing the leaves from my jacket, a woman's voice called out to me. A voice I never expected to hear again. When I looked up, Minta Gray was waving at me.

"Hello, hello!" she said. "You're Cassandra's daughter. It's me, Minta. Minta Gray!"

I lowered my head, pretending not to hear her. It didn't work. Before I knew it she was standing in front of me.

"Hi, Minta. Nice to see you," I said and forced a smile. Although she seemed like a nice woman, I didn't want any reminders from Mama's time spent in the hospital.

"You're Olivia, right?"

I reluctantly met her eyes. "Yes. You have a good memory."

"Oh yes, I remember everyone. How's your mama doing?"

"She's doing fine," I muttered. "Thank you for asking." I lifted my hand to wave and walk away, but she followed me and continued talking.

"Cassandra and I became good friends in the hospital. You know both of us have experienced a lot of sadness in our lives, she with your daddy and me with my daughter. My daughter would have been your mama's age."

"Yes, I remember you mentioning that," I said. There were people on the sidewalk, and I kept my voice low, fearing she would say "Milledgeville" or "Central State Hospital." If she did, I could never go to the library again.

"I'll tell Mama you said *hi*," I said quickly and tried to leave, but she inserted her arm in the crook of mine and nearly dragged me inside the library.

"Let me write down my phone number again. Maybe Cassandra lost it. I could really use a friend these days."

We were in the main room now. Minta sat down at a reading table. She opened her pocketbook and dug around in what resembled the inside of a trashcan. She pulled out a card and said, "Oh, this'll do," and wrote on the back of an appointment card. She placed it in my hand and closed my fingers over it. "Please have her call me, won't you?"

"Sure," I said. "Have a nice day."

Although I was relieved she'd gone, I couldn't help imagining her and Mama together. How could two mentally ill people hanging out together be a good thing?

Before I slipped the card in my pocket, I read the other side of it. It had an upcoming doctor's appointment written on it. I sure hoped she memorized the date because there was no way I was giving Mama the card.

I headed for the librarian's desk and then followed her instructions to the right shelf, pulled out the SAT-prep book and headed for the checkout. But the book was a lot bigger than I expected. I didn't think I could carry it home while driving a bike. Though it would take a while to read and more than one trip to the library, for the first time in years, I had nothing to rush home to. I figured I would stay and study. Only when my eyes began to ache, I returned the book to its spot and headed for home.

Just as I pulled Luke's bike from the bushes, I saw Monica and Tuck coming down the sidewalk, laughing and holding hands. I turned my head, pretending I didn't see them and started peddling trying to keep my focus off them.

Also, like with Minta, I couldn't get away unnoticed. Monica bumped her shoulder against mine nearly knocking me off the bike. In a sing-song voice she said, "Spelling Slut."

This didn't surprise me. I knew it was Monica who had written that note all along. I also knew she needed a dose of her own medicine. But it would have to be someone else who gave it to her. I had enough to deal with making sure Mama got hers.

CHAPTER 19

The Easter break was almost over and Uncle Bradley hadn't returned with Luke. Although he called and asked if it would be all right if Luke stayed with them a little longer, Mama began pacing the kitchen floor when she hung up, like she used to when she got upset.

"He's a liar! I knew I couldn't trust him. He wants to steal my boy."

CeCe looked up from her textbook. "Mama, he said he's only keeping him an extra week. He even offered to call Luke's teachers to get the work he'll miss. And you gave him the school's number."

"People do it all the time," I said. "It's the first time Luke's ever been away. Stop worrying."

Mama continued to pace. "I'm thirsty. Olivia, pour me a

glass of sweet tea."

"Yes, Ma'am." I poured her the drink and glanced over at CeCe.

Fear simmered on CeCe's face as it did in my stomach once again. I remembered how the doctor said Mama would never be completely well - the medicine would only help her remain functional. I wondered if she'd even been taking her medicine. At first, everything seemed great. Then she began complaining that it made her gain weight. And she'd prided herself on her girlish figure.

When she left for the bathroom, I rushed to CeCe and whispered in her ear. "I think she needs the other medicine. The one that makes her calm."

"Go get it," CeCe said. "It's in her top dresser drawer."

I rushed into Mama's room and tore through her top drawer. Then the drawer beneath. I went through every drawer in her dresser before I found the bottles, tucked under Mama's few winter sweaters. The bottle of Ativan was empty and the other bottle only half full. It looked like she'd stopped taking them. Judging from the dates, it looked like she hadn't taken them for weeks. And we had forgotten about Mr. Shimmering's instructions to make an appointment with Mama's new doctor.

I could almost feel CeCe's heart pound. Since she had

always taken care of Mama, Luke, and me, I knew she felt it was her responsibility to make sure Mama took her medicine.

"Maybe you can dump a couple of those sleeping pills in her tea again." I ran my fingers through my hair and took in a deep breath. "It worked before."

"Yeah, maybe I'd better," CeCe said. "And when she falls asleep, I'll call the doctor and order more."

Mama calmed down a little, but she didn't go to sleep. It wouldn't be until the next morning before CeCe could call the doctor. We got tired of waiting and went to bed with the hopes Mama would too.

* * *

"She's got to get to the doctor's office," CeCe said and left our bedroom to break the news to Mama, but she was gone. Her car, her purse, and her mink coat were gone too.

"Maybe she went shopping," I said, trying to deny what I knew we both felt in our hearts to be true.

"You know Mama would never shop on a Saturday morning," CeCe said while she rummaged through a pile of papers on the kitchen counter for clues. "She hates crowds."

Like a bad dream coming back, I saw the card that Minta had given me in CeCe's hand. She'd picked it up off the counter. But how did it end up there?

"I think I know where she is," I said, and pointed to the card.

CeCe stared at me waiting for an explanation.

"Minta. The woman I met at . . . at the hospital . . . I ran into her at the library. She kept babbling about getting together with Mama."

CeCe yanked the phone off the hook and thrust it and the card in my direction. "Call her."

The man who answered said he was Minta's son. He told me she and her friend left early this morning. He described Mama to a tee, and mentioned that Minta said she might be gone awhile.

"*Awhile!*" CeCe said when I shared the information. "She said she might be gone awhile. What does that mean?"

My stomach churned like spoiled buttermilk. "What should we do?"

CeCe rubbed her forehead between her thumb and forefinger. "Mama hasn't had a friend in a long time. Maybe it's a good thing."

"Sure," I said sarcastically. "If Westin sees Mama at her worst, we'll never see him again."

"Where do you think they went?" she asked.

I shrugged. "Not a clue." Pacing the floor just like Mama

does, I wracked my brain trying to figure out where she could be.

The phone rang. I jumped and grabbed it off the hook. "Hello. Yes? Hi, Westin. No, Mama's not here. When was the last time you saw her?"

"Not in a couple of days," he said. "She told me she was leaving on a trip today— to New York—I wanted to catch her before she left. Am I too late?"

"New York! Why would Mama go to New York?"

"Uh, she said something about taking care of family business. Is everything all right?"

I couldn't answer him. I had a strong feeling he *was* too late. I held my hand over the receiver. "He asked if everything is all right. What should I say?" I asked CeCe.

"Give me the phone."

"Hi, Westin," she said. "You know a little about Mama's condition, right? . . . Well, look, here's what we think might have happened." She explained about Mama not taking her medicine, and her being upset about Luke being gone to Florida. Then she said, "Do you think you can help us?"

My thumb slid underneath my upper eyelid. I gently pulled while I anticipated his response.

CeCe hung up and smiled wryly. "Pack your bags. We're going to New York. And Westin's taking us."

I let go of my eyelid - this time with only a small wad of mascara and a lash or two beneath my fingernail. "First, we have to call Uncle Bradley," I said. "You know she's angry about him keeping Luke. And since he's from New York, maybe he can help us figure out where she's gone."

CeCe called Uncle Bradley, and sure enough, he told us that Mama might have gone back to Daddy's old neighborhood.

"Where *is* his old neighborhood?" I asked.

She put her hand on the phone's mouthpiece and whispered to me, "Brooklyn. He said our great-grandmother lives there. Maybe she went to visit her for some reason. Get me a piece of paper, quick." She wrote down an address and phone number Uncle Bradley gave her.

I swallowed hard. As soon as she hung up with him, I said, "Brooklyn is huge. If Mama's not at our great-grandmother's house, how are we going to find her?"

"Pray."

CHAPTER 20

Westin opened his trunk and placed our bags inside and then opened the back door for us. We slid across the soft leather seats. I predicted a limousine might feel like this. The car reeked of new leather mixed with a strange-smelling tobacco. Not a speck of dirt lay on the carpet. I imagined I was a reporter going to New York on assignment, and Westin was my driver.

He turned on the radio and drove away. As we veered around the corner, I saw Miss Ruth crocheting while she sat on her wide-back chair. I waved. She glanced down quickly, pretending not to see me. I fought a giggle. *First the fur coat. Now a fancy car. I could only imagine the thoughts running through her head, preparing for a full-fledged gossip session.*

"I called your great-grandmother and introduced myself,"

Westin said. "She told me that indeed your mama had called and said she'd be coming with a friend for a visit. She sounded thrilled."

CeCe placed her hand on her chest. "Thank you so much for calling. I couldn't do it. I barely remember our great-grandma. It seemed strange to call her," she said. "Did you ask when she thought Mama would get there?"

"All she said was that she's on her way." He broke into a smile. "Not to worry, girls. We're on our way too. I believe God watches over those who can't do it for themselves."

I guess my initial thoughts about Westin were wrong. Even if I hadn't changed my mind, he was right. I had no choice but to have faith at that moment.

"How long will it take to get there?" CeCe asked

He glanced at his watch. "We'll be there sometime tomorrow afternoon. We'll have to stop overnight."

Westin pulled the ashtray open, took out a small wooden pipe and packed it with tobacco. He looked somewhat regal as he put the pipe in his mouth and lit it with a square silver lighter.

My eyes widened at the thought of spending the night with Westin. I whispered in CeCe's ear, "We're not sharing a room with him. I know he's been kind to us and all but—"

"Uhhh, Westin . . . we can sleep in the car," CeCe said.

He grinned. "Don't worry. You two will have your own room."

CeCe looked downward from Westin and murmured, "We can't afford a room."

I caught a glimpse of his eyes in the rearview mirror. "It's okay. I'll take care of it." True kindness streamed out.

"Thanks Westin," CeCe and I said simultaneously and sunk into the seat, relieved. I closed my eyes and drifted off to sleep.

* * *

Cherry tobacco smoke from Westin's pipe wafted through the air and woke me from a strange dream. I coughed and peered out the window. A sign read, "Welcome to South Carolina." We'd left the state of Georgia and though the circumstances were not part of my plan, a jolt of excitement filled my senses.

Westin cracked the window and pushed a cassette in the car stereo. Elvis sang gospel music as we drove up I-95. I realized what Mama meant when she said she had been the one to take advantage of Westin. Our own family wouldn't help us the way this man already had.

My heart felt at ease when I heard the voice of Elvis. I hadn't heard his gospel music since Daddy was alive. Whenever he took us on road trips, he played the same cassette. The song brought back a feeling I missed. A feeling I longed for. I felt God tugging at my heart while I listened to the words to *Peace in the Valley*.

No one spoke much, but by the time we stopped for a late lunch, it was clear that CeCe had warmed up to Westin too.

"How did you really meet Mama?" I asked. Subconsciously, I clutched my purse with anticipation, fearing he might share something too embarrassing to hear.

He chuckled and turned down the music. "You know your mama," he said. "I was driving home from work and noticed a beautiful woman strolling along the highway. She seemed confused. So pretty and all, I couldn't help but stop to ask if she needed assistance. When I rolled the passenger-side window down, she stuck her hand inside, unlocked the door, and jumped right in."

"She just slid right inside your car without saying a word?"

"Oh, no, she said plenty. She talked the entire ride home. Wouldn't stop talking." Westin cracked a smile. "Then she invited me in the house for a drink and got awful friendly, and quick."

He buried his head like a turtle into his shoulders. "I suppose that's a bit too much information to be sharing with you girls." In the rearview mirror, I saw his eyes soften. "I could tell she was in a bad way. I once knew someone like your mama."

He turned the music back up. The discussion stopped for a while, and CeCe and I fell asleep again. When I awoke, we were parked in front of a motel and Westin was gone.

I shook CeCe by the shoulder. "Westin's gone."

Bleary-eyed, she sat up, blinked a few times, and glanced around. "Bet he's in the office." She pointed to the front of the building. "He's probably checking in."

Seconds later he returned and opened the car door. "Come on girls, let's get you settled."

He carried our bags and unlocked the door to the room, and handed me a fistful of change. "There's a vending machine in the office if you get hungry. I'll be back bright and early." He clapped his hands. "I'll have the main desk give you a ring." He gave CeCe the key. "Sleep well. We'll have your mama back in no time."

"Thank you, Westin," both CeCe and I said.

CeCe placed her hand on his arm. "You've been very kind."

With a smile and a nod, he disappeared into the room next door. CeCe pushed the door of our room open and we tossed our bags on the beds. Two full beds with a nightstand and a TV on top of a dresser completed the room. It was clean and neat, and we were glad to be there. I plopped down on the bed closest to the door while CeCe ran for the bathroom.

I rolled around on top of the bed, then hopped up and grabbed my journal out of my bag and started writing. Somehow I thought that if I didn't write down what had happened today, I wouldn't even believe it myself a year from now.

By the time she walked out of the bathroom, I had my pajamas in hand and bolted in after her. I heard the television come on. A newswoman was talking about the weather.

"You did bring a coat, right?" CeCe asked. "It's gonna be cold tomorrow."

I cracked the door open and stuck my head out, removing my toothbrush from my mouth. "Yes, I brought the white rabbit. What better place to wear it?" I smiled, exposing a mouthful of green toothpaste.

"I brought the silver fox!" CeCe raised her eyebrows, grinned slightly and shrugged.

Wearing a fur coat searching for my Mama in New York City was the last thing I ever thought I'd be doing. I figured CeCe felt the same way.

I finished my nighttime ritual, I stretched out on the bed and waved my arms and legs on the silky bed cover as if I were making snow angels.

"Isn't this something?" I shimmied underneath the blankets and pulled them up to my neck.

CeCe slipped under the blankets as well, smiling with her eyes and a look of ecstasy upon her face as if she were posing for an ad for a queen size bed. "Nothing against you, Liv, but I long for the day I get my own bed."

"No kidding!" I said in agreement. "You've started snoring."

"You steal the blankets."

"I'm only trying to take back what I started with."

We both laughed, enjoying our freedom for the moment.

I sighed. "If Monica Bradshaw ever knew I shared a bed with my sister, she'd have a party to announce it."

"You won't have to worry much longer," she replied. "If I work extra hard, I might be able to graduate early, and I'll be out of here as quick as you can say, 'See ya, CeCe,' and you will have the bed all to yourself!"

My carefree moment came to a halt. CeCe had no idea how I hated when she talked about leaving. I couldn't imagine being on this journey without her. *What if Mama tries taking off again after CeCe's gone? It'll only be Luke and me. We can't handle it alone, I just know it!*

I changed the subject. "Hey, CeCe, how come you don't date anymore?"

She sat up and fluffed the pillows. "Who said I don't date?"

"Let's see. I've never answered the phone for you with a guy at the other end of the line. I've never seen you run out the door to get into a car driven by a guy. And, you never talk about guys. You're not *funny*, are you?"

She threw a pillow at me. "Maybe I don't want to talk about guys with my little sister. Did you ever think about that?"

I shrugged. "Pulleeze, I'm not so little, CeCe." I rolled my eyes. "Sure, whatever, but that only answers one of my observations." *Journalists must be very observant.* "What about the others? What about the phone calls and dates?"

She stared down and began picking at her fingernails. "I see guys at school. We go out for lunch, and sometimes dinner. Only I don't tell them where I live, and I don't give them my phone number. If you give 'em too much, they'll want more. That'll only complicate things. I told you, I'm out of here soon. I don't need a guy interrupting my plans."

I wanted to plug my fingers in my ears and yell, "NO, YOU CAN'T GO," but she had every right to pursue her dreams after fending for us all these years. Selfish guilt spiraled down upon me each time I thought about delaying CeCe's future so I could pursue my own, but it wasn't all for me. It was for Mama too.

"Well, at least you're not *funny*," I said.

She whipped her other pillow at me.

I tossed the pillow back and turned up the volume on the TV.

"See if you can find a New York station," she said.

I began switching channels and stopped to view the news. The anchorman discussed the sad economic state of the country then changed the subject to the benefits of the latest wrinkle cream. Within another few seconds, he moved on to the next subject.

He said, "Today, two unidentified women entered a nursing home in Brighton Beach, Brooklyn, and initiated a game of strip poker with some male residents. Obviously, someone wasn't doing their job." The anchorman chuckled. "By the time a staff member discovered them, the men were almost completely disrobed."

"I guess the women knew their game," the co-anchorwoman said.

"I think you're right," the anchorman responded. "According to our report, the only clothes *they* needed to put back on were their shoes and sweaters. The women left willingly, and the nursing home isn't pressing charges." Both reporters grinned.

The screen split to a clip of the women leaving the nursing home, escorted by what looked like two burly male nurses.

Our mouths practically dropped to the motel room floor.

"IT'S MAMA! Look at her, she's wearing a mini-skirt. And high heels! Where'd she get those clothes?" I said.

"Oh my gosh, look at Minta!" CeCe added. "I remember her being more reserved. If Mama didn't know her, she'd call her a floozy. An old floozy."

I couldn't answer. I was struggling to close my mouth.

CeCe shook her head from side to side. "I don't believe it. I didn't know Mama even knew how to play poker."

"Maybe Minta taught her," I shrunk down into the bed and pulled the covers over my head. I pictured the two of them playing poker in Central State, dressed in white hospital gowns at a round table. "I told you Mama's become promiscuous. She's like Jekyll and Hyde, only in a female way."

"At least we know she made it to Brooklyn," CeCe laughed.

I shot out from under the covers. "Oh, my gosh. I hope Westin didn't see this. There's no way he'd want to stay with Mama after knowing what she did. And he's been the first good thing that's happened to her since Daddy died."

CeCe nodded. I crawled back under the covers.

"I just hope she doesn't do anything else," CeCe said. "Now go to sleep. We've got a lot to do tomorrow."

And that was the last thing I heard.

CHAPTER 21

The phone rang at 5:30 a.m. I ran my hand across the bed for CeCe, expecting her to be nudging me to answer it. Then I realized I wasn't home.

CeCe answered the phone and hung up quickly. I wanted to lie in the enormous bed a little longer, but she ripped the covers off me and said, "Get up. Westin will be waiting for us."

Fifteen minutes later he knocked on our door.

"How'd you girls sleep?" He handed each of us a bag with donuts and a cup of tea.

I stretched and yawned. "Pretty amazingly, thank you." I glanced over at CeCe. "We haven't had our own beds in four years." *I can't believe I just told him that.*

CeCe nodded while her smile faded. She didn't like to share too much information and probably didn't like that I just did.

He displayed an understanding smile. Then out of nowhere he asked, "What happens if you eat yeast and shoe polish?"

CeCe rubbed her eyes. "Huh?"

I pinched her arm. "I think he's telling us a joke."

"Oh. Ummm, don't know." She yawned.

"You rise . . . and shine!" He clapped his hands and raised his arms in the air. "Wake up, girls! We've got a big day ahead of us. We'll be in New York in just a few hours, and we're gonna get your mama."

We tossed our suitcases into the open trunk, hopped in the car and took off. He adjusted his mirrors for the first few minutes. "Glad you slept well. We'll be doing a lot of walking."

"Walking? In New York?" I arched my right eyebrow. "Isn't New York like the biggest city in the world? How are we gonna find Mama on foot? And it's dangerous too."

While he answered, he twisted a Styrofoam cup of coffee into a holder in the console, and then packed his pipe with tobacco. "We won't be walking through the entire city, just certain areas." He lit the tobacco and puffed on his pipe. Then he cracked the window and blew the smoke out. "Some of the roads aren't fit for an automobile as fine as this."

"Yeah, we might be sucked into a pothole," I said. "Or we

could get barraged with windshield-cleaning fanatics. Or worse! Carjacked."

CeCe glared at me. "Where'd you hear all these things?"

"Jonzie's been to New York several times. She told me all about it." I wrapped my arms around my body. "Daddy told me too. He said some people make their living cleaning your car windshield. Whether you like it or not."

"Now, now, stop your worrying," Westin said. "Windshield washers are harmless, and I can't say I've ever known anyone who has been carjacked either." He smiled. "Once we reach Manhattan, I'm gonna drop this baby off in a parking garage. We'll be taking the subway to Brooklyn from there."

"The subway!" CeCe and I both said at the same time.

"We've never been on a subway," I said. "Aren't they even more dangerous?"

He took a sip from his coffee then placed it back inside the holder. "You'll be just fine. You're with Westin Barnes!" He held his head high and grinned into the rearview mirror at us.

Excitement and fear, my two closest companions, tugged at my insides again. I liked adventure - I yearned it. But the thought of Mama roaming around New York City on her way to Brooklyn with Minta frightened me to death. *Stop worrying,* I told myself. *She lived there for six years when she first met*

Daddy. She'll be all right.

I bit into my doughnut and sipped some tea to force it down my throat.

Westin slowed down to pay the toll before we traveled over the Delaware Memorial Bridge. "We won't be traveling entirely on foot, girls. We'll catch a few taxicabs too. Maybe we'll pass the nursing home Minta and your mama paid a visit."

I looked over at CeCe, saw her eyes were as wide as mine. I held my breath for a second. "Did you see the news?"

"Yessiree, I did—nearly choked on my pipe."

He pushed the Elvis cassette back into the stereo and we continued toward our destination. I whispered in CeCe's ear, softer than before to make sure Westin couldn't hear me, "What do you think he does for a living?"

"I don't know. Maybe he owns his own business or something." She squinted at the smoke swirling out the window. "Maybe a tobacco farm."

"Maybe he's a mobster," I said. "He's got lots of money and smokes a pipe and is very mysterious."

CeCe twisted her mouth into a cynical smirk. "There's no such thing as a southern mobster—and mobsters smoke cigars, not pipes."

"Sure there is. They're called Sicilians, they live south of

Italy."

CeCe rolled her eyes. "You need to get out of Landon. You're more than a few books short of the Landon Library."

When I ace the SAT test, and get a scholarship, everyone will see how smart I really am! And I will get out of Landon. I elbowed her in the side. "Shut up. I'm not stupid."

"You're not stupid, but southerners and Sicilians aren't the same."

I turned away. "I know that. I'm just being funny! You have no sense of humor!"

CeCe continued staring out the window and ignored me. Westin turned Elvis down a notch and said, "I own a real estate firm." He turned the music back up.

CeCe and I stared at each other and covered our mouths to stifle our giggles.

After talking for another hour or so, we fell asleep again. When I woke up, I smelled something similar to rotten eggs. "Eeeew, what the heck is that smell?"

"We're in Elizabeth, New Jersey," Westin said. "Stinkiest city in the Armpit State."

I waved my hand in front of my face. "What is it?"

"Factories."

"Daddy said New Jersey was a nice place," I said as I

pinched my nose closed.

"Oh, there are some wonderful places in New Jersey, the shore towns especially. But the turnpike in Elizabeth isn't one of 'em. In just a few minutes, we'll be going through the Holland Tunnel and we'll be in New York."

"Does it smell better than this place?" I asked.

"Yup, most of it anyway."

I sat up straight and paid detailed attention to my surroundings.

"CeCe, it's the Statue of Liberty," I said, pointing out the window. "And the Empire State Building!"

"Maybe I'll come here instead of Hollywood," she mused. "Actresses have more opportunities here . . . with Broadway and all."

There she goes again. "We need to find Mama," I said. "Stop talking about leaving, will ya?"

She frowned, and the light in her eyes disappeared.

I didn't mean to make her feel bad about leaving. It just scared me. And being scared about the condition in which we might find Mama was about all the fear I could take in one day.

Westin announced our surroundings as we drove through the city streets. "This is Chinatown," he pointed. I saw signs with Chinese writing along storefronts.

"Little Italy, right over there," he said and smiled. "Lot's of good food here!"

We drove through all the places I'd heard of but had never seen before.

He pulled down a street filled with restaurants in Little Italy and drove up a ramp into a dark parking garage.

"Okay girls, it's time to depart from luxury for a while. We need to refuel our bodies. We'll get lunch, then it's onto the subway and then Brooklyn."

The tiny restaurant reeked of garlic and wine. White linen towels hung on each waiter's arm. They filled our water glasses without asking, and placed more forks at the side of our plate than we'd normally made use of in an entire day at home.

I ordered chicken parmesan. Mama used to make that for Daddy when she felt like cooking. She still made it for us on special occasions. CeCe ate a salad and nibbled on bread from the basket in the center of the table. Westin ate something that resembled baby octopus. He called it calamari. It smelled good, but when he asked me if I wanted to try it, I declined. He simply smiled and kept right on eating.

After lunch, he paid the check, and we walked toward the subway. It was chilly, but not too chilly. Fog emerged from manholes covering the sidewalk. Vendors selling everything you could imagine lined both sides of the streets. I could've walked around for a year and not gotten bored. All sorts of aromas filled the air. One smell in particular caught my attention.

"What's that smell?" I asked Westin.

He lifted his chin and sniffed. "You mean the nuts?"

I inhaled deeply again. "Is that what it is?"

We stopped at a corner stand. "They're roasted chestnuts," he said.

CeCe and I stood next to him while he purchased some. I continued to take in the resonance of the city. Although I wasn't sure I liked the aroma of roasted chestnuts, it wasn't a scent I'd soon forget.

He held the paper bag tight and shook it. "Chestnuts are a tricky nut to roast. You need to slit 'em before you roast 'em, or they'll explode." He nodded in a serious way. "Also, when you crack 'em open, you need to make sure you check for dark spots. You don't want to eat the dark spots."

"Why not?" I asked.

He grimaced. "It's no good. It'll make you sick. You can still eat the nut, but first you've got to scrape the bad part away—kind of like pruning roses—only with roses, new ones will grow and take their place. That doesn't happen with nuts."

"Hmmm, seems like a lot of work just to eat a nut," I said.

"Yeah, maybe, but they're worth it."

The man behind the counter handed Westin his change, and he held the bag in front of me.

I reached in the bag and took a handful, cracked one and dug inside it with my fingernail. I popped the contents into my mouth. "Pretty good," I said.

"Told ya. Here, have a try." He handed the bag to CeCe.

"No thanks, I'll pass."

He shrugged. "Okay, maybe another time."

The light on the corner turned green and we skipped across the street with the montage of people attempting to beat the light before it turned red again. My eyes darted back and fourth watching the cars and the people pass by. Women dressed in business suits wore sneakers. Others wore mini-skirts, fur coats, and high heels. Jewels on their fingers and wrists flashed as they waved their arms in the air, hailing taxicabs. Homeless men and women rolled grocery carts filled with their belongings.

When we approached 42nd Street, Westin said, "Turn your head."

"Why?" I asked. I'd heard 42nd Street is where all the famous theatres are. I soon realized many other theatres could be found there too - the kind with triple X's posted across the marquee. Grossed out, I stuck to CeCe like a shadow. Westin walked with purpose, and followed behind us like a bodyguard.

"Y'all ready?" he asked a few minutes later, and stopped walking.

We stood at the top of a stairway of what looked like the entry to the bottom of the earth.

"Let's go." He grabbed CeCe's hand, she grabbed mine, and we walked down the steep stairwell. He approached an attendant behind a glass booth, and I heard him order tokens through a glass window. CeCe and I followed him closely, pushing through the turnstile. I was about to have my first subway ride.

Moments later we stood alongside train tracks and waited. The brakes screeched, startling me. I'd never heard anything so loud. Hordes of people poured out, and we crammed in between the assortment of people before the doors clenched our bodies like *Jaws*. Every seat was taken. We stood in the aisle and grabbed onto metal triangles hanging from the ceiling.

"You okay?" Westin asked, peering at CeCe and me. "You look a little green."

"Who me?" I asked. "I'm fine. CeCe's the one who looks like she's about to lose her lunch."

Her almost-blue knuckles held onto the triangle waiting for the train to take off. And when it did, it moved like lightning chasing the wind. I pretended to be fine . . . until the lights went out. I squeezed CeCe's hand.

"What's going on with the lights?" I asked Westin.

The lights turned on again.

"It's okay. It happens all the time."

Not exactly the answer I hoped for, but at least they came back on fairly quick.

Packed with strangers reeking of cologne, smoke, body odor, and unfamiliar foods, the subway car sped through the tunnels while the lights continued to flicker on and off. Each time they went out, I feared that when they returned, CeCe and Westin would be gone and I'd be alone.

The conductor hit the brakes and I lost my grip of the triangle, nearly landing in an old man's lap. Westin caught me just in time.

"This is our stop," he said. "Come on, we're almost there."

I almost skipped down the sidewalk. "I can't believe I'm gonna meet my great-grandma. I can't believe I *have* a great-grandma."

The light in CeCe's eyes told me she was excited too. "I wonder what she's like," she wondered as she puffed smoke rings with the frosty air. I tried too, but they came out in little cotton balls.

"Hold up, girls," Westin said.

We both turned around. He held a piece of paper in his hand and looked up at the house we were standing in front of.

"This is it. This is your great-grandma's house."

CHAPTER 22

C racks ran along the sidewalk toward the front steps of the gray stucco house - one of many that lined the block - close together with narrow alleyways in between. CeCe and I followed Westin up the steps. He knocked on the door with a fist bound in a rich leather glove. The cool air bit my face and hands now that I'd stopped walking. The fur kept my body warm, but I hadn't brought a scarf. I couldn't wait to get warm.

A black and white cat hopped onto the windowsill and peered through the curtains, but no one opened the door. He knocked again. We heard the noise of a creaking floor just inside the door. A peephole cover clicked opened and an old woman's voice said, "Who's there?"

"Ma'am, it's Westin Barnes. We spoke on the phone last

night. I'm a friend of Cassandra's. I'm out here with her daughters. Your great-granddaughters."

About five locks unlatched before the door finally opened, and a thin wrinkle-faced woman topped with a pile of hair with white roots bleeding into its hay color appeared. "My goodness, you're Jimmy's girls." She patted my face, and then did the same to CeCe. "Come in."

We walked tentatively into the gloomy house and took in our surroundings.

"Let me look at you." She stepped back and viewed us from head to toe, shaking her head unintentionally. "You're both beautiful. You remind me of your father," she added, staring at me. "Carnegie, you're the spitting image of Cassandra, but with Jimmy's eyes."

CeCe looked embarrassed. "Uuh, it's CeCe. No one ever calls me . . . Carnegie."

"Oh, dear, don't be so disgusted. I suppose Cassandra felt that way too when my grandson suggested they name you after me. At first, we called you Carnie, just like me. After Olivia came along," she nodded in my direction, "*she* named you CeCe."

"Thank God," CeCe said under her breath.

"You should thank me," I whispered, then grinned.

In response to what we'd said, the woman shrugged. "What can I say? Having no brothers, my mother felt the need to pass down her family name. But if you're happy with CeCe, then CeCe it is." She smiled. "The two of you sound like your mother too. I always loved that sweet southern accent."

She pointed to Westin. "Can I get you something to drink?"

"No, thank you, Ma'am."

"Aaah, a Southern gentleman," she said. "We don't get many of them around here." She scratched her backside and her polka-dotted housedress moved up and down, giving us glimpses of the top of her knee-highs. I found this amusing and I noticed CeCe did too. After the long ride, I guess we needed to release a little tension and we were enjoying a moment of silliness. I was glad to finally catch CeCe away from her serious mood.

"How about you girls?" she said. "Would you like some hot chocolate?"

I covered my mouth to stifle my giggles and glanced over at CeCe, who said, "Yes, Ma'am."

We followed her into the kitchen.

"Sit down. You must be exhausted."

"I don't mean to be rude," Westin said. "But last night you said Cassandra was here. Where is she?"

She turned on the faucet and filled the teapot. "She took her friend Minta down the corner to get a bagel." She turned off the water and placed the pot on the stove.

"Cassandra said she hasn't had one in fifteen years. She said Minta *never* had one. Everybody needs to try a New York bagel, don't you think?"

She'd said "New York bagel" as if it were equal to lobster and caviar. I thought it somewhat odd.

We listened while she made polite conversation as we sipped our hot chocolate, which was wonderful after being out in the chilly air. After we finished, she ushered us into the living room.

"Go ahead, make yourselves comfortable. I'll just be a minute in here."

The plastic-covered couch could only get so comfortable. I got up and eyed the place over. Pictures of people I assumed were my family members covered the tops of each cherry wood end table and filled the curio cabinet. Pictures of Daddy too when he was a young man. Everything looked antique, but in perfect condition. The room had an odor of beef stew and Ben Gay. I figured our great-grandmother must have been about eighty years old.

"Where is our grandma . . . and our grandpa?" CeCe asked Westin.

Westin rubbed his eyes like he was tired. "Your mama told me they passed away some time ago." He yawned. "She said your grandma didn't like her much. She didn't want your daddy to marry her. That's why he took her back to her hometown in Georgia. She'd only been here going to college. She told me after she married your father, your great-grandma was the only one who treated her well."

I found it strange Westin knew more about my family history than CeCe or me, and I wondered why Great-Grandma hadn't asked about Luke. Didn't she know of him?

"Why did she come here – now - after all these years?" CeCe asked.

"Cassandra's been babbling about the past a lot lately. I guess she figured your great-grandma would pass soon and felt the urge to see her. But I also think it's about your uncle taking your brother with him to Florida. "

Our great-grandma re-entered the living room and sat down in an old recliner. "Now that's better," she said. When she smiled, a full set of freshly bleached dentures that hadn't been there before took about twenty years off her age. I could tell she felt much better about herself from that smile. I smiled back, and then asked, "Do you know we have a brother too?"

"Of course I know about Luke." She slipped her hand

inside the pocket of her housedress and pulled out a picture and handed it to me. Luke stood next to Uncle Bradley and Mickey Mouse. The smile on his face said it all.

"Bradley sent me this last week," she said as tears welled up in her eyes. "He's a handsome boy. What a shame Jimmy didn't get to live to see him grow up."

I cleared my throat. "Not to be rude, Ma'am, but . . . do you know why Mama came here?"

"Please, call me Grandma." She took my hand in hers and squeezed it. Her hand felt like a silk glove. I wanted to caress it. "Your mother came to me because of Luke and Bradley."

"What do you mean," CeCe asked, looking confused.

"It seems as if your mother thinks my dear grandson and his bony wife Belinda don't want to return Luke."

CeCe gasped. "What!"

"Well, Bony Belinda can't have any children of her own, probably because she doesn't eat enough to feed the poor thing. I know I'm bony too, but I've always been that way. Belinda makes herself that way on purpose," she added, and frowned. "Anyway, Bradley figured that even though Luke's almost grown, he's still family, and he could be like a father to the boy. But he didn't intend to keep him for good - just another week."

CeCe's eyes bugged out. "No wonder Mama stopped

taking her medicine. She thinks Uncle Bradley's going to steal Luke. *They* sent her off the deep end this time."

Great-Grandma gave a casual wave of one wrinkled hand. "Don't worry. He'll give him back. The problem is Luke doesn't want to come back. As for your mother?" She sighed again. "I'm sorry to break it to you, but she went off the deep end ages ago.

CHAPTER 23

"You mean Mama was quirky, even before Daddy died?" I asked.

"Cassandra's always been 'quirky,' as you say." Great-Grandma whispered this, as if Mama might walk in at any moment.

"Actually, your father met your Aunt Nadine first. The three of them attended the same college, but Jimmy didn't know your mother in the beginning. She came out here a year after your Aunt Nadine did. Cassandra was very smart. But by the end of her first semester, college life became too stressful for her. I don't know all that happened, but she began hearing things the professor denied ever saying. At first we believed her. But then it started happening with everyone."

"You mean Mama's had episodes before?"

She smiled at me. "Is that what you call them these days . . . episodes?"

The three of us didn't answer, just nodded and waited anxiously for her to finish the story.

"Not long after that, your Aunt Nadine introduced Jimmy to your mother. Who told Nadine that your father said he liked her better. Your father swears he never said that. But he did say he thought it," she chuckled. "Eventually, he dropped Nadine and went with your mother."

"Nadine was angry, to say the least. Your grandma –my hardheaded daughter - was just as angry. She wanted Jimmy to marry Nadine. Your daddy said Nadine wasn't the marrying kind. And that he wanted a family . . . and . . . how did he say it? Oh yes, he said he wanted a family and a simple woman. Well, he got a family, but your mother was anything but simple. I mean, she was in a certain sense, but Cassandra's mind is very complex."

I clenched my hands in my lap, but released them, realizing that Great-Grandma actually had approval in her voice when she said that.

"Jimmy's parents stopped speaking to him once he married her," Great-Grandma continued. "Your Uncle Bradley tried to break the two of them up on behalf of his parent's wishes, but it didn't work. Instead, the whole family fell apart. Cassandra didn't return to college and the two of them eloped one night. Not long after, Carn . . . I mean, CeCe came along, and then you, Olivia."

She pointed at me and smiled. "Jimmy went to college during the day and worked part-time nights hauling boxes into trucks, while your mama stayed in the apartment they rented with the two of you. When Jimmy finished college and realized his parents weren't going to change their attitudes about your mother, he brought you all to Georgia."

It was a lot to take in, so it was a few moments before I asked, "I can understand Aunt Nadine being mad at Mama. Mama took Daddy away from her. But . . . if Mama stole Daddy from Aunt Nadine, why doesn't Mama like *her?*"

Great-Grandma rubbed her hands on her apron. "Well, I guess Cassandra was afraid— afraid Nadine would come back one day and charm your father away, like she did. Or maybe it was because of those quirks she has. She once told me she heard voices tell her to keep Jimmy away from Nadine."

I jumped in and said, "Actually, we found out she's not just quirky," I said. "Mama has mental illness—it's a disease you know—lots of people have it.

"It makes her paranoid. She also hears things no one else

228

does. The doctor gives her medicine for it. Mama needs to take it every day. The doctor says if she has stressful situations, it can act up. But if she takes the medicine, it won't be so bad. Only problem is . . . she stopped taking it."

Great-Grandma shook her head. "I guess they didn't have the medicine back then. But she had Jimmy, and he was all she needed."

Just then, Mama and Minta walked through the front door.

"My, my, looks like a family reunion," Mama said as she wiped a spot of what looked like cream cheese from the corner of her mouth. Minta stood next to her wearing a fur coat similar to the one Mama was wearing, but much older. "What are y'all doing here?"

I went right back to being speechless and I guess CeCe did too. Mama had disappeared without even leaving a note. And we came all the way to New York to find her, worried the whole time. And she was acting like we'd just gotten home from school!

Westin spoke first. "Cassandra, we were worried sick about you. You can't just up and leave without telling anyone."

CeCe threw her hands up. "Westin's right, Mama. And New York? What were you thinking?"

"Minta never had a New York bagel before. I wanted to be

the first to treat her to one."

"A bagel!" I said sharply. "You left us alone with no word to bring Minta here for a *bagel?* You never wanted to take us here when *we* asked." I felt my face begin to heat up and I knew I had to remain calm. But I was so angry.

"You haven't been taking your medicine," CeCe said. "If you had, you'd never do this to us. You have no idea what you put us through." She folded her arms and turned away from Mama.

"That medicine makes me sick," Mama blurted.

"How did you get here?" Westin asked.

Mama placed her hand upon her heart completely changing her tone. "Why, we took the train of course. You know I don't like to fly, and old Cherry Bomb wouldn't have made it past Atlanta."

"It was grand." Minta's eyes beamed. "We had our own train car and they served us breakfast, lunch, and dinner. Even saw a movie!"

"Why didn't you tell anyone where you were going?" Westin asked Mama. "I would've helped you—"

"I don't need any help." Mama flicked her arm in the air. "I'm taking charge of my own life. I want y'all to leave me alone. I get Luke back and everything will be fine."

"We'll get Luke back," Westin said. "Bradley and his wife don't want to keep him. They just want to be a part of his life. They know he's your boy."

"They tricked me," Mama said, and her lighthearted expression disappeared. "I had a feeling. An unsettling feeling in my gut. The same feeling I tell my girls not to ignore. Why did I ignore it?"

She began to cry, her mascara running down her face. Minta handed her a tissue from her purse and Mama dabbed at her eyes.

"It'll be okay," Minta said, rubbing Mama's back.

In that instant I realized Mama really came to reach out for help. She *did* fear losing Luke, but her mind was so jumbled up she couldn't keep everything inside it in order.

"Listen up!" Great-Grandma said. "Everything's gonna be fine. I'll be right back. I'm going to make a phone call to Bradley." She headed upstairs.

Trying not to be obvious, I walked back to the tiny foyer. CeCe followed. Both of us tried to hear the phone conversation from the bottom of the steps. We could see Minta strolling around the living room, checking out the pictures. Westin reached out and took Mama's hand but she pulled away. It must have hurt him that she was acting so distant toward him. He'd done so much for us. If it wasn't for him, I don't know what CeCe and I would've done to get Mama back.

Minta started yapping about the sights of New York and how she planned to come back again with her son. A few moments later, Great-Grandma toddled downstairs, her steps slow and careful even after she wasn't on the stairs anymore. Somber-faced, she said, "Bradley will bring Luke back . . .just as soon as he finds him."

Mama stopped her pacing ritual. "What do you mean, *find him?*" She said this in the same deep voice she'd used in Central State when she told CeCe and me to take her home. I'd hoped never to hear that tone again.

The edge of sanity suddenly seemed like home to me as well as it did Mama. I envisioned all my plans drifting away like a paper sailboat. Even the SAT test, which was next week, seemed only a faint hope now. I couldn't think past the moment. Why did Luke *do* this?

Fighting tears, I thought, *maybe the way I'm feeling is how Aunt Nadine felt about Grandma and Grandpa. Maybe that's why she went away to college and never went back to Georgia. Will CeCe do the same thing?*

Mama started pacing again. She began speaking quietly at first, addressing the voices in her head. Then she became louder -

they must have as well. "My face is burning," she suddenly yelled, and ran to the kitchen. CeCe and I followed.

She opened the refrigerator and took out a carton of milk. With her hands shaking, in haste, she poured some into a glass, dipped her fingers into the milk and wiped her fingers over her face.

"What are you doing, Mama?" CeCe asked, watching in horror.

"The milk cools the fire. The vitamins heal the skin that covers the mind." She repeated this several times.

"It's happening again," I whispered, miserable once more. CeCe only nodded.

When we spoke, Mama only seemed to hear pieces of what we said. I was frustrated. I didn't know what to do but try to reason with her. CeCe didn't seem to have a clue either. Once again I remembered what I'd learned about Mama's illness. *You can't reason with someone when they're in a psychotic state, and the more you try, the more frustrated the both of you will become.*

Back in the living room, I told Westin, "We need to get Mama to the hospital. She needs her medicine."

"But she'll never agree to go to the hospital," CeCe interjected. "And she won't take the medicine. It makes her feel bad."

"Maybe the doctor will try a new medicine," I said. "Remember what Mr. Shimmering said. We still have to get her there."

An idea came to me. "You can do it again!"

"Do what?" CeCe asked.

"Put sleeping pills in her sweet tea." I stared up wide-eyed at her. "When she falls asleep, we'll put her in the car and take her to the hospital."

Blank-faced for the first time, Westin didn't say a word. No jokes, no answers. No suggestions of what we should do for Mama. Could she have pushed him too far? Was her baggage too heavy for him to continue to hold? Did he think we'd *all* fallen over the edge? I only had time for a quick prayer and I hoped with all my soul God would answer.

"I need to go out for a bit," he said. "I'll be back soon." He looked at each of us with sadness in his eyes before he walked out the door.

Mama didn't even notice he said goodbye. I feared he wasn't coming back, and although she didn't say a word, I knew CeCe feared the same thing. She had grown dependent on him just like I had on her.

CeCe whispered in Great-Grandma's ear and they headed

into the kitchen. She turned on the water and filled the teapot. A few minutes later I heard ice crackling and the spoon stirring against the glass. CeCe handed a glass to Mama, who continued to stand in front of the open refrigerator looking oblivious and wiping her face with milk.

"Mama, put that down," CeCe said. "I'm making you a glass of sweet tea."

"Thank you, you're very kind," she said, like she'd never met CeCe before. She sat down on the plastic-covered chair in the living room.

CeCe went over to the sink and filled Great-Grandma's teapot with water. I didn't know if she would have the ingredients to make the "sweet tea," but I also knew CeCe would do her best to improvise. I also knew CeCe had that bottle of Sominex in her pocket.

Once the tea cooled, CeCe brought the glass to Mama who took it from her hand. "It's a little different than we make at home, Mama, but it's still good." Mama took small sips. Time moved like an old 45 record played at 33 speed. Finally she finished, and we waited. And waited.

At last her eyes became heavy. CeCe placed a pillow behind her head, and moments later, Mama was snoring softly.

I hugged my sister and leaned my head against hers. "You

are the smart one."

*   *   *

I tried to think positive. *Maybe Westin didn't scare off that easily.* But if he did, who could blame him? I wondered why this wealthy real-estate man cared so much about Mama. Perhaps the same Southern charm she used on Daddy worked on all men. Besides getting Mama well, it was all I could hope for.

CHAPTER 24

M ama woke up with a vengeance. "I'm not going with you. I'm staying here 'til Luke comes back."

"Mama, Luke will be going home," I said. "To *our* home in Georgia. If we're not there, he'll worry. If we're not there, Uncle Bradley will take him back to Florida," I added, hoping to get through to her.

Mama gazed around the room as if she hadn't a clue where she was. Silently she examined each one of us as if she were searching for something.

Without warning, she raced to the front door, flung it open, and bolted for the street. The brakes of a white station wagon screeched but couldn't stop before it hit her. Her body didn't fly, but *transcended* to the other side of the road.

I took off first. CeCe followed. Minta lagged behind,

yelling, "Oh, no! Oh, no!"

Mama lay limp on the side of the street. I lifted her arm and felt her pulse. She was breathing, but blood trickled down the side of her face.

"Mama! Mama, can you hear me?" I called out.

She moaned. Strangers from the neighborhood surrounded us.

"Please, someone call an ambulance," CeCe shouted.

Within minutes, an ambulance arrived. EMT workers lifted Mama onto a gurney. She was awake now but didn't fight them or squirm to get loose. I think somewhere in her right mind, she knew she needed to go. A female EMT worker tried talking to her but Mama seemed catatonic.

CeCe and I jumped in the back and waved to Great-Grandma and Minta as they stood like fragile relics on the brown patch of grass.

"Tell Westin," I shouted to her, then couldn't help thinking, *if he comes back.*

The EMT waved at me to hurry. I pulled my head back inside and she slammed the door. We drove away into the crowded streets of Brooklyn. I watched Great-Grandma and Minta stumble back toward the house.

The ambulance weaved in and out of traffic as anger filled

my thoughts. We had been so close to going home, and Mama screwed everything up again. *Why?* I asked God. He didn't answer.

We followed the EMTs inside the hospital. Complete chaos enveloped the emergency room. Nurses ran back and forth directing people. I prayed that Westin would appear and make everything okay. Hours passed and people came and people went, but Westin never showed.

Finally a room became available for Mama and a doctor walked over and spoke to CeCe and me in a thick foreign accent. "Your mother has a concussion, a broken leg, and some bruises. She will be fine. She's very lucky. However, her mental state is not so good. She is on a strong sedative."

"When can she get out of here?" CeCe asked. "We need to get back home—to Georgia."

The doctor glanced at Mama's chart. "I am sorry, but I cannot answer that yet. It depends on how she responds to the medication."

Here we go again, I thought. I'd grown as dependent on Westin as I had on CeCe. I wished I hadn't. It was easier not to expect anything than to expect it and lose it.

"Where could he be?" CeCe said. "I'm sure Great-Grandma told him what happened."

Once again, the two of us hadn't eaten, and we slept on and off through the night on uncomfortable chairs in the waiting room. With no money, no car, and no idea what Great-Grandma's phone number was, we were completely lost in a whirlwind of confusion.

* * *

"They're over there," a woman's voice said, and a muffled voice answered her.

I lifted my head from CeCe's shoulder and rubbed my eyes, but I couldn't see anyone.

"Right here," she said, this time her voice was closer. I could see it was a nurse speaking.

I glanced up. Westin stood in front of me, next to the nurse. With a smile, he held out a bag of doughnuts.

"I . . . I didn't think you were coming back," I said.

"You should know me better than that." He reached down and gave my cheek a gentle pinch.

CeCe woke up and rubbed her eyes. "Thank you," she said as she stood and hugged him.

"You must be hungry. Have a doughnut and let me see what's going on."

CeCe and I stared at each other and closed our eyes, and then looked up toward Heaven.

Westin returned a few minutes later. "The doctor gave her a different medicine, and he's hopeful she will respond quickly. She needs to stay here for a while before she can go home. Y'all can fly back. I'll get the plane tickets and your Uncle Bradley and Luke will meet you at the airport in Atlanta."

CeCe and I both gasped. "Uncle Bradley found him!" I squealed.

Westin nodded, grinning. "Bradley found him, *and* your brother's ready to come home. I'll stay here in New York until your mama's— as soon as she's well enough, I'll bring her back."

"Where'd you go, Westin?" I said and turned away feeling out of line for asking. After a minute, I forced myself to meet his eyes again.

"I had to take care of some business. And then I had to find someone to drive my car back for me." He gave CeCe and me a nod of reassurance.

I believed the part about the car, but I had an inkling he needed some time to decide if he was in or out of this family. I tried, but I couldn't think of any words big enough to describe how happy I was to know he was in.

CHAPTER 25

CeCe and I got back on a Friday. Uncle Bradley met us at the airport with Luke, and Minta's son was waiting for her. Uncle Bradley drove the three of us home to Landon, and a week later Westin returned with Mama - a new and improved Mama, but sporting a cast on her leg and using a pair of wooden crutches to help her walk.

Meeting Great-Grandma had been awesome. And it was a relief to have Mama back. For me, I just wanted to get back to my life, or at least start working on one. Sure, Matt and I were over, and the same with Tuck and me, but I still had to focus on my future.

I'd missed the first week back at school after spring break. When I told Bessa and Jonzie all that had happened they were stunned.

"Sorry you didn't get back in time for the SAT test," Bessa told me.

"I can take it in the fall," I said.

"Bessa says you're gonna be a newswoman!" Jonzie blurted.

"I said *journalist*, Jonzie."

"You'd make a fine newswoman."

I smiled at them both and raised my chin. "Thank you."

Matt sauntered by and I caught sight of the tattoo on his shoulder, peeking out from beneath the sleeve of his gray t-shirt. "Hey, wait up," I said. "Haven't seen you in a while. What you been up to?"

He shrugged. "Nothing much."

"What ya got there?" I asked, and pointed to his upper arm. I wanted to see if he had indeed removed my name.

He pushed the sleeve up and I moved in closer. I could see the letter *O* - for Olivia - had been transformed into a rose. The same with the letter *A* at the end of my name, and the *I* was now an *E*. The heart was changed into a bouquet of roses, and now, the word *LIVE* written inside.

"Wow, it came out nice," I said, and ran my fingers across it. "Your cousin is certainly creative." *Who would've thought* I'd *come up roses out of all of this?* I smiled.

"We could still go out some time," he said and winked.

A flush of heat ran across my face. I stood quiet for a moment, and a memory of our "almost" night flashed through my mind. As strong as my attraction was for Matt, I decided I had something stronger to hold onto. I smiled once again and said, "I'm pretty busy these days, but thanks for asking."

He shrugged off my rejection with his ever-cool attitude.

"Well, I've got to get to class," I said, not wanting another awkward moment to pass by. "See ya."

"See ya," he said back and strolled away.

I smiled to myself at the thought of his tattoo. *Live*. That's exactly what I planned to do, and for *me* this time.

* * *

I heard the sound of Westin's car outside and knew they were back from dinner. A few minutes later he and Mama strolled inside. She smiled a lot lately, but the grin plastered on her face was wider than usual.

"I have something to show you," she said. "But first, I have to tell you how it happened." Still grinning wide, she shook her head back and forth. "Y'all know this man and his unusual sense of humor, right?" She directed her eyes to Westin, and we all nodded.

"Well, we were sitting in the front seat of his car, and he

was holding his pipe." She deepened her voice like Westin's. "He said, 'Cassandra could you get my bag of tobacco?' Now, I didn't think anything odd about this. I do it for him all the time. But when I pulled the bag out of the glove compartment, I saw what I *thought* was a piece of glass inside. I said, 'Oh my goodness, how the heck did that get in here?' You can't be smoking glass. So I gently dug inside the bag to pull it out, and wouldn't you know . . . it wasn't glass at all."

"What was it, Mama?" Luke asked curiously.

We all waited to hear. But Mama didn't say another word. Instead, she pulled the glove off her left hand and displayed a diamond ring the size of Atlanta.

When she held her hand out in front of us, I sniffled and wiped sudden tears from my eyes with my sleeve. That ring was pear-shaped sunshine sitting in a platinum setting.

The three of us stood up at the same time. CeCe and I coldn't hold back our tears, this time they were tears of happiness. More than we'd experienced in a very long while. Luke's eyes gleamed the way they did before Daddy died.

"So, is it okay with you?" Westin asked. "Can I be your step-daddy?"

The heaviness that lay upon my chest for so long rolled away like the rock in front of Jesus' tomb. I grinned so wide I thought my cheeks would bust and wrapped my arms around his neck. "Yes Sir!"

* * *

Westin wanted Mama to fill the month of December with happiness so she would no longer dwell on Daddy's passing. Mama agreed and the wedding was set for December 4th. Minta and her son would be attending as well as Great-Grandma and Uncle Bradley and Bony Belinda. Even Grandma and Grandpa Cleveland would be there. Uncle What's-His-Name said he couldn't make it, and CeCe announced she'd be bringing a date.

After the church ceremony, the reception would be in the new house Westin was building for us. When he showed us the plans for the house, I nearly fell off my chair. It was beautiful and tremendous in size. It sat up on a hill overlooking an entire neighborhood. Monica Bradshaw's neighborhood. We planned to move in on the Saturday after Thanksgiving almost a year later.

I figured I might as well say goodbye to the only neighbors who'd ever given us the time of day, so I walked over to Miss Ruth and Bubbles Clayton's trailer to wish them a happy Thanksgiving. I giggled to myself, realizing they'd need to seek new entertainment once we moved on. Miss Ruth sat in her rocking chair like usual. Only the brace that had supported her neck for so long was gone. She stood up and held her head high.

"Olivia. I heard the good news."

How did she hear? I instantly wondered. It's not like we talked to anyone in Woodlane. Then again, since Mama was now on her way to marrying Westin, she practically shared it with the whole world.

Miss Ruth grabbed my hand. "I'm glad your mama's okay. I didn't want to be a nosy-body, but when I saw her last fall staggering toward the highway one night, I called the police. I'd seen her roaming around the park many nights, but this night, I was afraid if I didn't call, she might get killed."

"*You* were the one who called?" I said, surprised.

"I thought it was my Christian duty to help out." She nodded as if God himself commanded her to do so.

"Thank you," I said. "It's good to have neighbors looking out for us." I smiled inside and out and waved goodbye.

Back at home, I helped Mama get the food on the table and we all sat down to Thanksgiving dinner one last time. I couldn't have been happier - I think everyone felt that way. Still, I knew that Mama had this awful disease and she would always need someone to watch over her. I pushed the thought out of my mind and gazed out the window to the spot where a turkey once lay sacrificed and buried. So much had happened in just one year. Our family and whole world had changed, but some things remained the same.

I finally took the SATs, but it didn't matter anymore whether I got that scholarship. Westin said he'd pay for my education. Even so, I hoped for high enough scores to have my pick of colleges. I thought I might go to college in New York with CeCe. She changed her mind about Hollywood, and to my disbelief, Aunt Nadine invited us to visit her there. The question came in a card she sent asking about Mama, and when CeCe and I told her, Mama didn't seem nearly as upset as we'd expected.

Everyone sat around the small kitchen table and I pulled up a seat.

"Olivia, will you say Grace?"

I tilted my head and gazed at Mama surprised by her request, but after a moment, I nodded. "Sure."

I bowed my head. "Thank you, Lord, for this wonderful meal and the hands that prepared it. Thank you for our friends and family. Thank you for answered prayers and the new life that lies ahead. Amen."

"That was real nice, Olivia," Mama said.

"Let's eat," Luke added.

Forks clanked against our new china dishes and everyone gobbled up the good food. While I ate, I thought of the all the people who touched our lives this past year. People I never knew existed, people I'd never thought capable of helping, and people I feared were out to get us. I finally understood how God held the whole world in His hands.

I smothered gravy on a slice of turkey to make it more edible. I never did like turkey much.

"Pass the potatoes, please," Luke said, and his voice cracked a little. Now thirteen, a small patch of whiskers caught the mashed potatoes he shoveled into his mouth. I decided to leave the lecture that he needed to start shaving to Westin.

"Olivia, I forgot the sweet tea," Mama said. "Mind getting out the pitcher and pouring me a glass, please?"

"Sure, Mama," I said, and got up from my seat and did what I'd done a thousand times that year - a year that rushed by like a crowded subway train flying through a dark tunnel. Lights on. Lights out. Lights on again.

And a glass of sweat tea.

END

Sweet Tea Recipe

Ingredients
10 regular sized Lipton tea bags
Fresh, filtered water
1½ cups of sugar
¼ teaspoon of baking soda

Instructions
Bring 4 cups of water to a boil, remove from heat and add tea bags.
Let tea steep for about 10 minutes.
Remove tea bags and add sugar to hot water.
Stir until sugar is completely dissolved.
Add baking soda and stir again.
Pour tea and sugar mixture into large pitcher.
Add 12 cups of ice water and stir until cooled.
Serve over ice.
Makes one gallon of sweet tea

Acknowledgements

To my children, Zane and Alyjah. Your support, help and enthusiasm has meant so much to me.

To my friend Annie Alberta, who's always claimed to be my biggest fan.

Linda McElroy, Joanne Malley and Donna Correll for always being there to listen and read my manuscript over and over and offer me your talents and endless patience.

To the awesome writers on the Verla Kay Blueboards. You are the most amazing group of writers, critiquers information-filled, fun, caring people I have ever known.

A special thanks to Kay Pluta, Angela Ackerman, Natalie Dias Lorenzi and Diana Greenwood for critiquing my book in its early stages and offering their wealth of knowledge and talent.

To Verla Kay for her great dedication to writers and illustrators and creating the Blueboards. You are a monumental asset to SCBWI and anyone who has stumbled upon your well-organized haven of information and support.

My Sister, Denise for being a character inspiration from a middle-child's perspective, and just being my sister.

To Pat Florio, our meeting one another was serendipitous for sure!

To Larissa Spathis for totally getting my vision for a book cover.

To Jerry, for totally getting me.

And to God, for blessing me with words to paint everlasting stories.

About The Author

Wendy Lynn Decker lives in the historic town of Ocean Grove, New Jersey. After raising her two children, a son and daughter, Wendy pursued her dream of becoming an author. She published her first book, **The Bedazzling Bowl, (2006)** an inspirational chapter book for middle-grade readers. When she is not writing, she is a singer/performer for adult communities throughout New Jersey.

To learn more about her please visit her web site at: www.wendylynndeckerauthor.com

About NAMI

Mental illness affects everyone. Nearly 60 million Americans experience a mental health condition every year. Regardless of race, age, religion or economic status, mental illness impacts the lives of at least one in four adults and one in 10 children across the United States.

People living with mental illness need help and hope: they need a community that supports them, their families and their recovery.

Because mental illness devastates the lives of so many Americans, NAMI works every day to save every life.

NAMI is the National Alliance on Mental Illness, the nation's largest grassroots mental health organization dedicated to building better lives for the millions of Americans affected by mental illness. NAMI advocates for access to services, treatment, supports and research and is steadfast in its commitment to raise awareness and build a community for hope for all of those in need.

NAMI is the foundation for hundreds of NAMI State Organizations, NAMI Affiliates and volunteer leaders who work in local communities across the country to raise awareness and provide essential and free education, advocacy and support group programs.

What is mental illness?

A mental illness is a medical condition that disrupts a person's thinking, feeling, mood, ability to relate to others and daily functioning. Just as diabetes is a disorder of the pancreas, mental illnesses are medical conditions that often result in a diminished capacity for coping with the ordinary demands of life.

Serious mental illnesses include major depression, schizophrenia, bipolar disorder, obsessive compulsive disorder (OCD), panic disorder, posttraumatic stress disorder (PTSD) and borderline personality disorder. The good news about mental illness is that recovery is possible.

Mental illnesses can affect persons of any age, race, religion or income. Mental illnesses are not the result of personal weakness, lack of character or poor upbringing. Mental illnesses are treatable. Most people diagnosed with a serious mental illness can experience relief from their symptoms by actively participating in an individual treatment plan.

Learn more about **treatment and services** that assist individuals in recovery.

Find out more about a specific mental illness:

http://www.nami.org

Coming Soon……..

COME AS YOU ARE

CHAPTER 1

I stared at my half-brother while he lay in an economy-style casket, something you might find on discountcoffins.com, if there is such a thing. I had been writing to Jack for six months, but I hadn't seen him since Belmar, four years prior. No idea how he died or how he ended up in an adult prison before he turned eighteen, a million questions ran through my mind.

Kristopher squeezed my hand. "You sure you're all right?"

"It's just . . . he looks so hard." I turned away from the casket.

"Sorry, Abril, but it's not like he's been living in Boca." He wrapped his arm around me, and I edged my chin above his shoulder. Although not a couple, Kris and I were close and lately I'd been fighting the feeling to get even closer. He gave me a gentle squeeze. I glanced up and noticed people staring. I'd grown accustomed to the stares. How often do you see a seventeen- year-old girl with purple hair accompanied by a blind guy and his guide dog?

Chloe brushed up against me as if she could feel my sadness. Though a seeing-eye dog, it seemed as if she had many special senses. I scratched her silky head.

Jack must have received his fair share of gaping eyes in life as well as death. A tattoo of an eagle encompassed his bald head where his long strawberry-blonde hair had once been. He looked old, worn, defeated. I glanced around the sparse room, and still didn't see anyone I recognized, nor did I hear anyone mention Jack by name.

My gaze lingered on the only flower arrangement on a pedestal in the corner of the room. I wonder who brought it, or who sent it? I continued to scan the room and listened to the blend of voices hoping to hear something about Jack.

"He wasted his whole life…"

"Things like that happen all the time…"

Things like what? Just last week I received a letter from Jack telling me how excited he was that I'd be coming to visit him.

Everything in my life was exactly where I wanted it to be. I couldn't imagine ever again being in a position where I had no control. Even though Jack screwed up his life, and I didn't know how, his letters told me he regretted what he'd done. That in itself drove me to want to visit him.

I leaned into Kris and whispered in his ear. "This place is so depressing."

"Is there any other kind of funeral home?"

"This doesn't even look like a funeral home. You'd think there would at least be a couple of pictures of Jack on the mantle or something to remember him by. How strange!"

Kris stood frozen for a moment and took in a deep breath. "About twenty, I'd say."

"Twenty what?"

"About twenty people are here."

I counted heads, "You're right. I'll never understand how you do that."

"Maybe they didn't decorate because they were in a rush. Maybe this is one of those one-stop shopping places—but for funerals and weddings—like in Vegas." He chuckled softly then whispered his "Kris-like" explanation in my ear. "When everyone leaves, the undertaker whips off his tie, douses his hair with gel, puts on an Elvis cape and conducts a wedding ceremony."

I placed my hand over my mouth to cover the grin and then

wiped the spray of saliva from my ear. Kris had a tendency to spit when he whispered, "You're crazy." I whispered back. "How do you know what Elvis looks like, anyway?"

"Everybody knows what Elvis looks like." Kris lifted his chin, moving his head around like a white Stevie Wonder.

I couldn't resist a good sense of humor. That's what drew me to Kris, and it's what kept me writing to Jack, despite his frequent moodiness. Sometimes Jack spewed venomous paragraphs at me as if he were writing to someone he hated. Then he'd suddenly change the subject and write about music or a new book he'd read or he'd share a silly joke. At least I could count on his inconsistency to be consistent.

Kris and I moved along with the short line. The room was so small we could hear the muffled gasps from behind as people approached the casket.

Kris squeezed my hand. "You okay?"

"Yeah," I answered and patted his arm.

"Mostly old people here, right?"

"Why do you say that?" I scanned the room again, confirming his statement.

"This place reeks of Old Spice and Jean Nate´." He waved his hand in front of his nose to force the scent away. Chloe, his guide dog, sneezed and all eyes shifted toward her. "See, even

Chloe noticed."

"Behave." I gently jabbed him in the side with my elbow. I inhaled, nonchalantly. "It does smell a little like your grandma's house after one of her houseware parties."

"Uh-hum." Kris nodded. I stepped forward and he grabbed my hand moving along with me closely.

"Here." I patted a seat along the aisle. "Sit down, I'll be fine.

"You sure?"

"Yes, it's okay, really."

Kris moved toward the chair with Chloe. Wearing his designer sunglasses, he bared more resemblance to a rock star than a genius. His loose, honey blonde curls hung an inch below his collar and his creamy complexion didn't offer much chance of growing facial hair anytime soon. Actually, he was much too hot to be blind, and too blind to know I probably wasn't his type. It didn't matter anyway. I knew you shouldn't mix business with pleasure, and I did not want to risk losing what we had. Sight and Sound Music Studio was my ticket to freedom.

I followed the procession toward the head of the condolence line. Bleached-blonde hair and deep crevices encased Jack's mother's lipstick-caked mouth. Like an aged fashion model that spent too many summers on the beach, time had not treated her well. I'd only met her a handful of times, but I didn't recognize her.

The line moved again bringing me closer to Jack's mother. I dug into my pocket and grabbed my little, green security stone and clutched it tightly. Did anyone here really know Jack? Did he know any of them? I wished I had known him better.

So close to the woman now, I could hear the voices of each person claiming sorrow for her loss, and I had full view of the casket again. A tall, skinny guy wearing a black knit cap approached it. A half-moon of his face peeked out and he wore a pair of aviator sunglasses. I watched him as he observed. His blackish/brown ponytail hung down his back. He stood there longer than anyone else had, made a peace sign, and strutted out the door, bypassing the rest of the line.

Finally, someone who looked like he could have been a friend. But I figured he didn't know Jack's mother and only showed up to pay respects. I wasn't exactly sure what that meant, though. Did one pay respects to the dead or to their living? If it was to the living, then this guy didn't pay respects at all. If it was to the dead, how would they know; they were dead? I rubbed the stone between my thumb and forefinger.

The line moved again, and I stood face-to-face with the frail blond woman. I shoved the stone into my jacket pocket then reached out for her hand. "I'm sorry for your loss. I'm Abril. Do you remember me?" She didn't take my hand. I slipped my hand back into my packet and clutched my stone again.

"No. Sorry, who are you?"

Made in the USA
Charleston, SC
27 April 2014